TEENAGE FEVER

Thomas Mild

ISBNs
E-book: 978-1-971324-02-9
Paperback: 978-1-971324-03-6
Hardback: 978-1-971324-04-3

DEDICATION

FOR MY DAUGHTERS

CONTENTS

CHAPTER 1

Stockholm woke like a bruise: tender, careful, trying not to touch the parts that hurt.

A café on a corner along Hornsgatan had a spiderwebbed pane pulled tight with clear tape that caught the weak winter light and turned it into a wrinkled sheen. Someone had wiped the soot from the frame but left a thin, gray thumbprint near the handle, a fossil of last night. A stairwell two streets over still smelled faintly of smoke and melted plastic, and the doormat inside was gone, replaced by a rectangle of clean floor that made the rest of the hallway look dirty. A TV mounted behind a barista's head carried the morning program, and the anchors recited another shooting the way they read the weather: a high of three degrees, a low of one, one dead in Husby, two injured in a car outside a pizza place, no arrests. The barista, who used to turn up the volume for music videos, now kept it low, and people carried their takeaway cups past a strip of sagging crime-scene tape the way they stepped over puddles—without looking down.

The city had learned a new posture: chin tucked, eyes forward, keep moving. It wasn't denial so much as stamina. But even stamina frays.

At a crosswalk near Slussen, the pedestrian light clicked over to green and the little tick-tick-tick that guided the blind stuttered for a second, like a record catching on grit, then found its rhythm again. No one looked up. Somewhere, a clock that didn't belong to the morning had started.

∧∨∧

POLICE LINE DO NOT CROSS
POLICE LINE DO NOT CROSS
POLICE LINE DO NOT CROSS
POLICE LINE DO NOT CROSS
POLICE LINE DO NOT CROSS

Mandy didn't hear the first alarm so much as felt it: a thin whine that threaded into her dream of Hawaii and folded the beach like paper. She was barefoot, stepping off a hotel path toward white sand that looked too perfect to be real, the kind of sand people posted and filtered and captioned with seashell emojis. Palms leaned into a sky that had never heard the word March. She thought—ridiculous, impossible—*Was someone here with me? Dad?* The thought arrived like a shadow and ran ahead of her toward the water.

Her hand, under the blanket, fumbled for her phone on the nightstand and smacked plastic.

The screen lit her ceiling. 72:00:00. One second later: 71:59:59. The digits were too big, too red—more old clock radio than smartphone. For a breath she wasn't in bed at all; she was inside the numbers, watching them roll down, each click a tiny drop in pressure inside her ears.

She blinked hard and rubbed both eyes until the room blurred and sharpened again. The numbers were gone. The lock screen read 06:45. Mandy frowned. On school days she always set the alarm for 07:15. She squinted at the alarm icon in the corner, tried to remember if she'd changed it, then shrugged and sank back into the warm dent she'd made in the pillow. Maybe she'd hit *snooze* without seeing. Maybe she was still half-dreaming. She chased the hotel path like a dog chasing a car that had already turned the corner.

When the next alarm went off, it *felt* like a minute had passed. The phone glowed 07:15. She stared at it through lashes gummy with sleep and then jabbed *snooze* again and again, trying to force the hotel back. Five minutes. Five more. She could hear the ocean if she concentrated—something vast and kind that had nothing to do with tram timetables or cafeteria lines or homework that wasn't done. And with it, she could feel her dad. He was right there, right there with her in that sand, she could swear it.

71:59:59

On the sixth snooze she sat up with a jolt so violent the blanket slithered off her knees and her heart hammered as if she'd been running. "No. No-no-no." Today was the math test, first thing. If she missed it, she wasn't just getting a zero. She'd slide into that special group, the one where Stoffer and Ivan parked their restless legs and swapped gross jokes about girls and guns and bad splatter movies while pretending to learn. She could *feel* the smug look Stoffer would give her: *Welcome to the land of the doomed, Mandy.* Over her dead body!

She rolled out of bed and made for the closet, calves tight, mind already doing math that wasn't on the exam: shirts vs. pants, stains vs. stares, the overused camouflage of black on black. Safe choices. She tugged out her two winners and held them up like tarot cards to the gray light filtering through the blind. The fact that she had already worn both combos this week would not be lost on anyone with eyes.

"Damn not having a rich dad like Lilian," she muttered, working her legs into jeans with one hand while the other tried to find a hair tie on the desk. Lilian always showed up in clothes that still had crisp folds in the fabric, the chemical smell of *new* riding behind her like a cologne. Weekends in "the city" with her father had become code for swiping the black AmEx: sneakers, jackets, bags. The full costume. "If only I had two normal Svensson parents," she said to the closet, "like everyone else."

She paused, shame flushing her neck. Not literally everyone. And "normal" wasn't real. But still: two boring salaries for pointless, boring jobs, money that added up to summer cabins and actual vacations and a *clothing fund* that didn't bounce. She had the child allowance; it was all hers. But what did that matter when every week there was a new way to look poor if you didn't keep up?

How Mercedes managed was a mystery. *Her* mom didn't even hand over the whole allowance. Half the time there was barely food in the apartment. Maybe that was why Mercedes was so tiny. Guys noticed tiny. Guys liked tiny. The thought made Mandy's stomach flex with something dark and mean, and she shook it off, finding the hair tie under a worksheet and pulling her hair into a line that might pass for deliberate.

She grabbed her backpack, her phone, her lipstick. When she turned towards her bedroom door, for one second, stupid as a movie, she looked toward the window hidden by curtains and thought she'd see a tall shadow there. Her heart stuttered: *Was someone there? Was it... Dad?*

The idea hit like it always did: a fast punch under the sternum. It was over as fast as it came. Her grief over losing her dad felt like a phantom limb. She carried the weight of his loss even in his absence- especially in his absence. Maybe that's the price you pay when you lose someone so close to you: the stubborn sanity of believing they're still beside you, even when they never will be.

As she shook her head and made her way downstairs, she could hear the voice of the morning radio filtering through the kitchen walls, "...new bombing overnight... a stairwell in Sollentuna... residents report—" Normally, when she wasn't sprinting, Mandy would roll her eyes and nag her mother to change the channel. *Hello? It's called music.* Anything other than the drum of bad news that made you feel dirty after.

She was halfway to the front door when her mother called, "Hey! Breakfast!"

"I don't have time," Mandy said, windmilling her arm through the sleeve of her jacket.

"Wait! I'll make you a toast. You'll get sick if you don't eat." Footsteps. The shuffle of someone half-awake but trying.

Mandy stopped in the doorway and put her forehead briefly against the cool wood. The Vespa from next door revved outside, coughing out gas-tinged air through the gaps in the old windows. On the hallway wall was the photo she always pretended not to see. The little girl she was holding the hand of her favorite man with an open, joyful face. He was squinting into the camera as if the light had surprised him. As if there'd never be enough time to see everything he wanted to see.

She sighed and burst into the kitchen. Olle was already at the kitchen table while her mom quickly prepped her breakfast. He was small for fourteen, with pale wrists that somehow looked both fragile and busy, scribbling in a grid notebook with a mechanical pencil that clicked click-click when his thoughts got ahead of the lead.

"Time?" she asked, tapping the chair with anxiety.

Olle pointed at the microwave clock that read 07:33 and then at the oven clock that read 07:31, as if the two-minute disagreement was an interesting debate worth attending. "Microwave's fast," he said. "Oven's slow. The radio's between." He tapped his notebook. "I'm tracking it."

Mandy rolled her eyes and ruffled his hair, which he tolerated the way he tolerated rain: a thing that was happening to him. "You tracking the whole universe in there?"

He looked up just enough to catch her face and frown. "You have a little blood." He touched the tip of his own nose. "There."

She wiped under her nostrils with the back of her hand and it came away with the faintest pink. "Dry air probably," she said. She ran water over a wad of toilet paper and pressed it to the spot until it stopped being dramatic.

"Test today," she said to Olle and swung her backpack onto one shoulder. "Wish me luck."

"You don't need luck," he said simply. "You need to read the question twice before writing anything." He flipped a page. "And write your units."

"Thanks, Sheldon," she said, referencing the genius kid from Young Sheldo, making the name light so it wouldn't sting. Olle nodded like she had said his actual name. He went back to the columns of numbers and tiny arrows that flowed like a private river down the page.

Her mother appeared with a napkin-wrapped sandwich—two slices of toast pressed together so the butter wouldn't leak through the bag—and peered at Mandy's face, a tiny crease digging in between her eyebrows. "Are you okay? You look pale."

"Fine," Mandy said too quickly, taking the warm bundle. "Just... I think I dreamt about Dad." The admission felt like dropping a glass and hoping it wouldn't shatter on the tile. She tried to make it nothing with a shrug. "Yelp, mamma! I'm late."

She was already gone when her mother said, to the empty hallway, "Of course you are." She stood for a moment. "Fuck the universe," she muttered under her breath, without heat, like a toast to an enemy. She took a bite of the extra sandwich she'd made for herself and chewed as if it had never been complicated to swallow.

Mandy skidded socks-through-shoes to the door and the hallway and the stairwell that always smelled faintly of someone else's dinner and damp sneakers.

On the sidewalk, she pressed the crosswalk button and waited with two other people who were not looking at each other. The tick-tick-tick of the pedestrian signal was a nervous finger on a table. It stuttered again—one tiny hiccup—and then remembered how to be a metronome. Mandy looked up at the little green man and felt, absurdly, like he was sprinting faster than usual across his tiny street.

Get a grip, she told herself, and stepped off the curb.

The tram was a long, patient animal. It breathed a sigh of doors opening and took in a slice of the city. It smelled faintly of wet wool and that fake lemon cleaner no one believed in. Mandy found a standing spot by one of the thin poles and wrapped her hand around it, letting her weight drag her shoulders down until her spine popped. She saw herself reflected faintly in the opposite window: hair tied back into something straight, a mouth that looked like it didn't want to talk right now.

The doors slid open again and Mercedes slipped in sideways, as if the tram had asked her to dance and she had decided it was worth a song. She was small, all angles and energy, cheeks flushed from the run, a scarf trailing like punctuation. She fitted herself into the space beside Mandy and bumped their shoulders together like clinking glasses.

"You look like death," Mercedes said, delighted. "Did you sleep, or did you watch all eight hours of those makeup hacks again?"

"Night school in Hawaii," Mandy said, deadpan. "Very intense."

"Manifesting, girl," Mercedes said, widening her eyes like a cult leader. "You have to manifest. Step one: we walk past Bianca's boutique and absorb the vibe. Step two: we return after school and... inquire. Step three: the universe showers us with freebies for being iconic."

"Step three: security," Mandy said. "Their new hobby is *not* letting kids touch anything."

Anoth
Stair
Blas

"Okay, okay, micro-inquiry. *We* don't touch. Our eyes touch. Eyes are allowed to touch, right?" Mercedes waggled her eyebrows. "We're being subtle. Elegant. In and out."

Mandy laughed, which felt like drinking water she hadn't known she needed. "You and subtle? Name a more iconic duo."

Mercedes fluffed her hair that did not need fluffing. "I can be subtle. I am a specter. A whisper. A—what's smaller than a whisper?"

"A thought," Mandy said. "And you are not a thought."

"Rude but accurate," Mercedes said, pleased. She leaned her temple against the glass and made a face at her reflection. "You wore the black again."

"Spotted," Mandy said. "Points deducted for lack of fashion and extreme mediocrity."

"Points added," Mercedes said automatically. "It's... classic. Classic is *rich.*"

"Classic is 'I only own two shirts,'" Mandy said, but she smoothed the shirt anyway, as if she could press desire into the fabric, make it something else.

The tram slid along, doing its steady magic trick of turning distance into near. They passed a shoe store with a sign that looked like a mistake and then a florist that bravely kept tulips outside in buckets, their stems stuttered by cold. A billboard perched over a bus stop with the face of a politician who looked like a cousin who was asking for money. His mouth was set in the shape of *We are handling it*; the graffiti bubble someone had drawn on his cheek said *lol.*

They turned a corner and there was Bianca's—the aspirational mirror they couldn't afford. The windows were the kind that were not windows but glass performance stages. Inside were ferns that had never met dust and racks of clothes that had never been snagged, the hangers like silver smiles, the tags tucked just so. A little crowd had installed itself by the door, girls dressed like the idea of a girl that you had to pay a lot of money to meet.

Mercedes's breath fogged the window and she wiped a little circle with her thumb like a child. "She might be there," she stage-whispered. "She might be there in real life. In the wild."

"Bianca is never in the wild," Mandy said. "She *is* the zoo."

"Manifesting," Mercedes repeated, softer, eyes still on the door.

Mandy let herself look without flinching. The boutique did look like a different weather system. The kind where it was always nice and always new, where clothes weren't a problem to solve but a language you were born knowing. She tried to resent it and failed. It was too easy to want.

"After school," Mercedes said, peeling herself away from the glass. "We do a *micro*-inquiry. Or... a visit. 'Micro-visit' sounds like a disease." She turned to Mandy. "You in?"

"Depends," Mandy said. "On the math test. And on security. And on whether the universe wants us to be iconic today."

"The universe always wants us to be iconic," Mercedes said with conviction.

Mandy hid a smile in her scarf. "You and the universe should get a room."

The tram jostled as it crossed an intersection and reminded Mandy's stomach that it hadn't been convinced the toast hadn't been a lie. She put one hand flat against her belly, closed her eyes for a second, and let the sway rock her thoughts into a simpler shape. Numbers. Questions read twice. Units.

"Don't puke," Mercedes said out of nowhere, as if she had been in the same brain. "You know I love you but I will abandon you if you puke."

"I'm not going to puke," Mandy said. "That would be... deeply uncool."

"Iconically uncool," Mercedes agreed, and nudged her, gentle. "You okay, though?"

Mandy nodded, slow. "Just... tired."

"From Hawaii," Mercedes said, accepting an explanation that explained nothing.

The tram slid into the next stop. Doors opened. New people breathed in their quiet clouds and took their places in the choreography. An older woman in a down coat had the morning paper folded to a headline about explosions, and she looked at it the way you look at a hand you can't control. A boy in a blue hat played a game on his phone with the volume off, his face lit a little from below. Two men speaking Somali laughed softly at something one of them had said, the kind of laugh that felt like a secret handshake, and Mandy felt something in her shoulders unclench. The city was still the city. You could measure its pulse if you pressed the heel of your hand hard enough.

They rattled over a bridge. The water below was the color of a coin someone had left in their pocket through the wash. It moved anyway.

"Okay," Mercedes said, as if concluding a meeting she had called to order, "agenda item one: Mandy crushes math. Agenda item two: micro-visit. Agenda item three: we practice *subtle*."

"Subtle," Mandy echoed solemnly.

"Like a whisper," Mercedes said.

"Like a thought," Mandy said, and this time Mercedes didn't argue.

At the next stop, they would get off and spill into the school stream and take their seats and be the kind of girls who rolled their eyes in ways that didn't get them in trouble. Mandy would put her head down over the exam paper and do the thing Olle had told her to do, and maybe she'd get through without her stomach betraying her. Maybe today would be the day the city decided to be a place where things happened on purpose, not to you.

The doors slid open. They stepped down. The tick-tick-tick at the crosswalk stuttered once, then found itself. Mandy pulled her jacket tighter and followed her best friend into the morning, pretending the sound she heard wasn't inside her head.

CHAPTER 2

The next morning, at 05:41, the world had been extra dark in the specific way kitchens were dark just before the lights came on. Mandy had woken without meaning to, the kind of full-body start that made her fingers claw the sheet, a gasp in her throat like she'd been caught doing something. The phone on her nightstand had already lit. It was not her alarm. It was not anything she could swipe away.

70:00:00.

And then: 69:59:59.

She had tried to swallow and found her mouth dry and her heart loud. The numbers sat on the glass with a strange wrongness—too saturated, too crisp, too red, like blood seen under a blue light. The color made a tiny ache spark behind her eyes. She thought of the crosswalk tick stuttering yesterday, of the big clock in the metro station that sometimes skipped a second and then pretended it hadn't.

She told herself to look away. She did not.

The air in the room changed. She didn't know how else to say it. The dark got heavier and quieter, as if someone had pressed two palms flat to all the walls at once. Then the corner by the wardrobe filled with the shape of a man like a photograph developing in a tray. He wasn't transparent or glowing. He was ordinary, which made it worse: the specific jacket, the specific shirt, the way his hair refused to go where it was told. The way he took up the exact amount of space he used to take up when she was eight and he stood in the doorway to make sure she was sleeping and not reading under the blanket with a flashlight.

He didn't speak. He couldn't; she knew that without knowing how she knew it. He lifted his hand and pointed at the phone. That was all. A gesture like a dot at the end of a sentence. *Look.*

"Dad," she said, and it came out broken, like a word that had been left out in the rain.

She blinked. In that blink, the corner was empty, the air thin again, the bedroom exactly as it had been built—cheap, warm, not haunted. The phone showed her lock screen. 05:41. Notifications dozed in a little stack. There were mismatched socks on the floor and a worksheet about linear equations trying to find a pencil that wasn't under the bed.

"Okay," she told herself out loud because sometimes it helped to have a voice break the spell. "Okay, okay, okay."

She got up because lying down made the room tilt. In the mirror above the sink her face looked like it had been left in a backpack. She pinched color into her cheeks the way she'd seen Mercedes do, which did almost nothing and made her feel human anyway. The overhead light was too white and too kind.

It let you see all the places where you were not the person you pretended to be.

"Blue light," she said to the girl in the mirror, as if they were discussing a science project. "Brain freak-out. Grief." The word *grief* was like a cough. "Just... a screen doing a weird thing." She rinsed her mouth and spat and rinsed again until the taste of sleep was gone.

She wanted to check all the clocks in the house and hold them all up against each other and ask them to stop arguing by even a second so she could make sense of it all. Instead she padded back to bed and pulled the blanket up to her nose and told her heart to stop being so dramatic. She would not tell her mother. She would not tell anyone. She didn't want anyone to worry about how dad's loss was eating at her soul to the point she was starting to get hallucinations. She would get dressed. She would go to school. She would be fine. She would bury the panic under mascara.

ᴧᴠᴧ

By second period the school had settled into its usual noise, a steady surf of locker doors and laughter and squeaking sneakers, the kind of soundtrack that sounded normal if you didn't listen too carefully to what people were actually saying. Someone in the corridor was live-reporting a fight that had happened last night in a stairwell—"no, for real, like, actual smoke, my cousin filmed it"—and someone else was promising to send the video if the Wi-Fi would stop dying for five minutes. A guidance poster peeled from one corner above the water fountain, asking *How are you, really?* The answer, in black marker, was *tired.*

Mandy and Mercedes claimed their usual patch of bench by the big window that looked onto a rectangle of gray sky and a birch tree that tried its best. The girls did what they always did: arranged themselves so they looked like they were killing time on purpose. Backpacks turned into footstools, phones into mirrors, bodies into posed ease. Performing normal.

"Okay," Mercedes announced, slicking a finger under one eye to chase a fleck of mascara, "how hard was math on a scale of one to I hope I never have to do numbers again?"

"Read the question twice, write your units." Mandy said it in Olle's even voice and then shrugged. "Hard-ish. I didn't cry."

"Growth," Mercedes said solemnly, then ruined the solemnity with a grin. "Math is a stupid language anyway. Who decided x had to stand for anything? I want to talk to that person."

"Probably dead," Mandy said. "Of old subtraction."

"Good," Mercedes said, leaning back until her spine clicked and exhaling like a cat in a sunbeam. "I'd fight a dead man. I could win that."

Mandy smiled and let her shoulders drop. If she looked at Mercedes, if she tracked the tilt of her head and the angle of her knees and the way her thumbnail traced a little moon on the bench varnish, she could keep her brain from replaying the morning like a jump scare.

Do not think about it, she told herself. *I just need more time to process this new reality after Dad's death.*

The corridor thinned as a class bell rang somewhere and pulled a river of bodies toward doors. For a few beats, the world was students who didn't have to be anywhere yet, which meant they were rich in a currency that felt more expensive than money. Mercedes used that little bubble of time to fish a slim vape from the sleeve of her jacket and hide it in her palm. She didn't draw; she just looked at it, like a charm.

"I hate going home," she said, casual, the way someone would comment on the weather. "Like, actually hate. I'd rather sweep the courtyard with my hair."

"I know," Mandy said softly.

"There's this chair," Mercedes went on, voice flat as she kept her gaze on the far wall so she didn't have to look at Mandy and see a face that cared. "In the hall? It's just… a chair. Except it's not. It's a… pile. Unopened envelopes and overdue everything. A little mountain of *you've failed at life, congrats.*" She twisted the vape in her fingers. "Every time I walk past, I feel like the chair is… looking at me. Judging the life I live. Like a person."

"Burn the chair," Mandy said. It came out a joke, but her stomach pinched. "Arson solves everything."

"Arson! We stan arson," Mercedes said, and laughed, but the laugh broke in the middle. "Mandy, she sleeps, okay? She comes home and she sleeps. Or she drinks and then sleeps. Or she smokes and then sleeps. Coffee, red wine, cigarettes. Those are the food groups. Bread sometimes. Butter if I'm lucky. 'Hello, my darling,' she says, like she remembers, and then it's like I'm the couch and she's the blanket."

Mandy didn't say she knew. She didn't say that every time Mercedes came to her place and her mom made enough pasta for two, the look on Mercedes's face did something complicated in her throat. She just slid her foot sideways so their ankles touched. "You could live with me," she said for the hundredth time, and meant it for the hundredth time.

"I basically do," Mercedes said. "Then I go home to that… air. It's like the apartment has mold but for feelings." She lifted a shoulder. "It's fine. I'm fine. I'm a survivor."

"You are," Mandy said. She believed it in the way people believe in weather reports: with faith and with a spare jacket in their bag just in case.

"I mean," Mercedes said, pulling her mouth sideways, "school is better than home. Which is saying a lot because school is also school. But the attendance thing—" She stopped, fiddled with a loose thread on the sleeve of her hoodie, then decided to either tell the truth or lie and chose the truth. "Sometimes, I just want to burn the world down."

Mandy snorted. "Because… *we stan arson.*" She could see it, as if in a flashback. Almost like a vision. How easy it would be for the world to end, at least their own, considering how the violence ran down every street. A quick explosion, the heat in their legs as they would run afterward, breathless and raw, and then... black.

Mandy shook her head. *The fuck was she thinking?*

The corridor filled again and spilled again, and they both got up to make it to the next period. The birch outside shifted and showed its white scars. A paper airplane, expertly folded, sailed from one end of the hall to the other and landed in a trash can with a satisfaction that made three boys cheer. A poster for a poetry slam flapped, as if clapping.

Mandy checked the time and looked away quickly, a reflex. 10:07. She slid the phone into her pocket before her brain could mistake them for anything else.

Don't think about it, she told herself again. *You are okay. People hallucinate sometimes and it goes away.*

Now, by the lockers, she reached for her combination without thinking, muscle memory doing what brains sometimes couldn't. She spun left, right, left, and the lock stuttered under her fingers as if it had forgotten the sequence and then remembered. Mercedes, balanced on one foot to adjust her sock, said, "Okay, so micro-visit later? We go together. Don't ditch me."

"I would never betray you for anything... other than maybe some chocolate cake," Mandy said, smiling as she tugged the locker open. Inside was a mess of books and a sweater that still smelled like the detergent they'd bought on sale.

It happened in the thin space between looking and not looking. The fluorescent tube above them hummed and then, clicked, slid a fraction of a tone lower. Mandy felt the change in her teeth. The corridor sound thinned as if the room had taken a breath and decided to hold it. The air around her wrists prickled with the tiny pins of static you got when you took off a sweater too fast in winter.

On her phone screen in her hand: 57:12:59. She hadn't touched the screen. It wasn't the lock screen. It wasn't anything but red. Then 57:12:58. Then 57:12:57.

No.

She lifted her head. The man was standing by the end of the metal locker run, not far and impossibly far, as if the length of the corridor had stretched and shrunk at the same time. The exact man from 05:41. She said "the man" because this man could not be who she wanted him to be. Even if she could see the exact clothes from the day that had been cut out of her life like someone tearing a picture from a magazine too fast and leaving white teeth in the paper where the tears had been. He lifted his hand and pointed at the phone. He didn't hurry. He held her eyes as if he had fought the universe itself to be able to see them. Mandy found her breath and steadied it because if she didn't, she would start crying and then people would put hands on her and nothing would be okay again.

"Mand?" Mercedes said, turning her face toward her with the beginnings of concern knitting her eyebrows. "Hey?"

Mandy blinked. He was gone. The air snapped back to its previous density, as if someone had taken their hands away from the walls. The fluorescent tube jerked back up a half tone and returned to its old bad self. At the end of the corridor a boy laughed too loud and slapped his friend's shoulder. The metal door of the locker next to hers slammed and made that same hollow bang that lockers made in every school in every country. The hallway clock mounted above the double doors read 10:13, then, as she watched, 10:18. Within a blink, 5 minutes had gone?

Did I pass out? Zone out? Is that why I am seeing things like a dream? OR AM I LOSING MY FUCKING MIND? Her brain was a mess of thoughts, running too rampant to hold. She wanted to scream. Bolt. She was going crazy, she could feel it. She'd heard of cases where grief pushed people past the edge of depression and into insanity—but she never thought she'd be one of them.

"Mandy." Mercedes's hand was on her elbow now, steady, like a person tightening a knot in a rope. "You look—" She searched for the word. "White. Whiter."

"I'm fine," Mandy said, even though the word rang false to her own ears. She reached up to push hair off her face and her knuckles brushed her nose and came away red. Of course. Not dramatic. Just... visible.

"Shit," Mercedes said, instantly in motion. She twisted, grabbed a wad of paper towel from the dispenser by the girls' bathroom door, thrust it into Mandy's hand, shouldered them both out of the lane of student traffic with her small animal certainty.

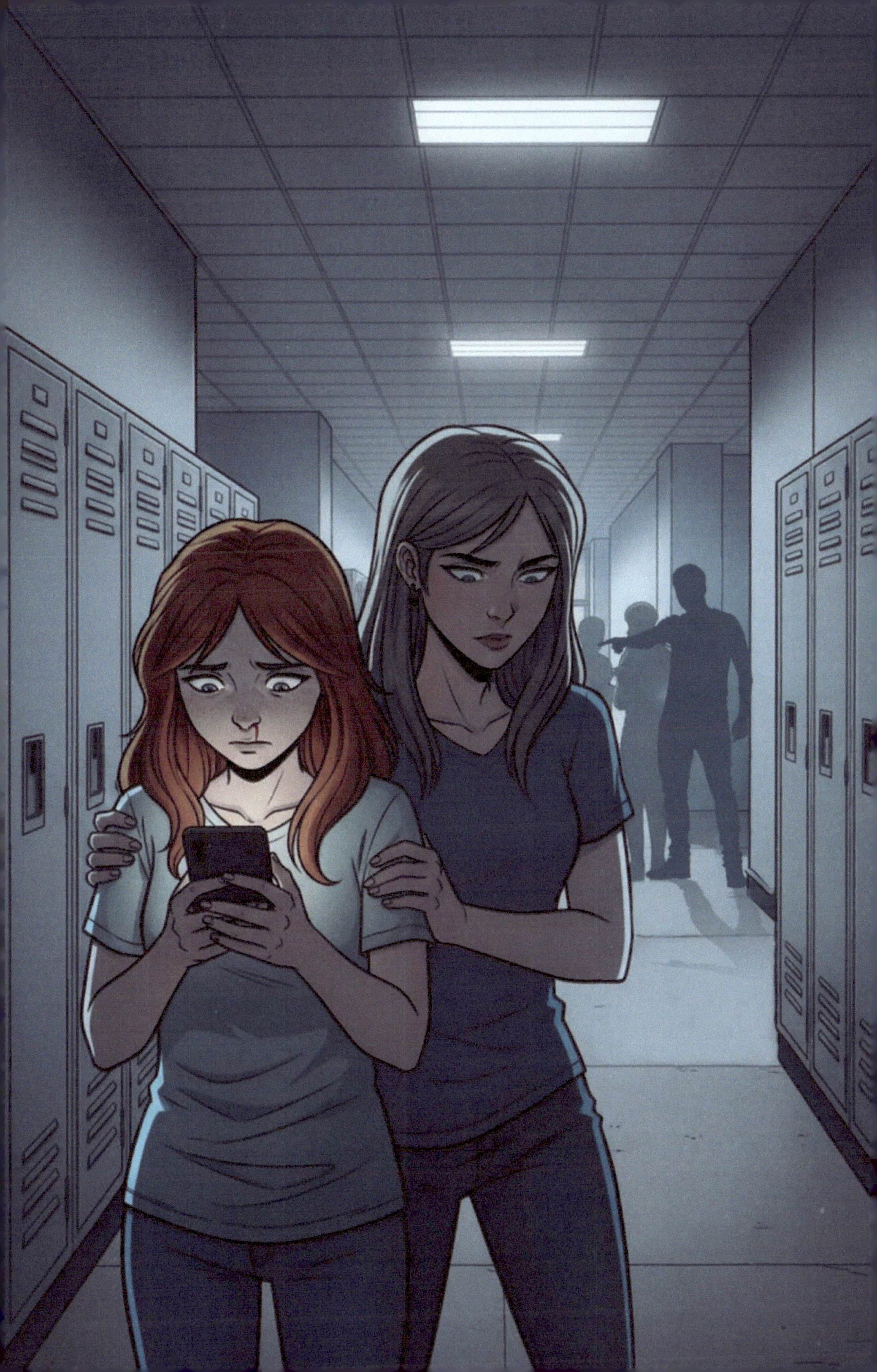

"Tilt your head forward. Not back. You remember the blood thing? Head forward. Pinch."

Mandy pinched where Mercedes told her to pinch and tried to breathe around the feeling that her bones were humming. The blood stopped being a flood almost immediately because it hadn't been one. It was a dot that wanted an audience. She could handle a dot.

"Better?" Mercedes asked. She sounded like she was also asking *Are we okay? Am I about to have to punch the universe?*

"Better," Mandy said. She blinked again. The clock stayed politely on 10:17. Her phone was... her phone. Messages. A notification about a sales email from a store she could not afford even when the email screamed SALE in capital letters. A battery percentage that didn't match how tired she felt.

She turned the phone face down in her palm, like the way a person might put a hand over a mouth to stop words from escaping.

"Okay," Mercedes said, switching gears without grinding them, because she could do that when she needed to. "So. Micro-visit after school. We do the glide-by. We practice being shadows. Subtle like—what?"

"A whisper," Mandy supplied.

"Right," Mercedes said. "But hot. A hot whisper."

"That's just breathing," Mandy said weakly, and Mercedes grinned, and the normal world, obliging, rolled forward an inch to meet them where they were.

A teacher walked by and said, "Ladies," like he was reading the word off a cue card. A girl from their class—with the comma eyebrows—shot them a look that judged and measured and then moved on to fresher prey. A boy in a hoodie stepped on his shoelace and almost fell and laughed at himself before anyone else could.

Mandy pressed the paper towel to her nose one last time and then, because she could not help herself, slid the phone up just enough to see the time. 10:18. It looked like a regular number on a regular screen.

"Bathroom?" Mercedes said, already half-turned.

"In a minute," Mandy said. "I'm good."

Mercedes studied her for two seconds, then nodded. "Okay. We have ten minutes till science class, keep moving. If we don't keep moving, we turn into furniture. Now, *that's* real science."

"Totally science," Mandy said, and even that small joke felt like a miracle, like the first step off a shaky ladder onto a floor that seemed like it might hold.

Mandy did not look up at the hallway clock again. She didn't trust it yet. On her tongue, behind the taste of blood and cheap paper towel, she could still taste the syllable she hadn't said out loud in the corridor: *Dad.* She swallowed it because it didn't help anyone to put it into the air. She pressed her phone flat to her thigh and felt its warm square through the pocket, like a living thing.

CHAPTER 3

Throughout the week, Mandy found herself going through the same motions of everyday school life amidst her emotional turmoil. By the time physics rolled around, the school had eaten and exhaled two more periods. The corridor smelled like pencils and someone's too-strong body spray and the ghost of recess. Mandy and Mercedes drifted with the crowd toward the science wing and aimed for the back row, where you could pretend you weren't listening and still hear everything.

"Bet you five kronor the cafeteria is doing vomit soup," Mercedes said, bumping Mandy with her shoulder as they squeezed through the door. "It's a tradition. If it's gray and it gloops, they serve it."

"You owe me from the last bet," Mandy said. "It was not vomit. It was... beige."

"Beige is just the French word for vomit," Mercedes said, solemn as a priest, and slid into a chair like it was a throne. She tugged her hoodie sleeves down to cover the little burn-holes near the cuffs that she claimed were from a dryer and Mandy suspected were from nerves and too many late-night cigarettes when the apartment was too quiet.

Ms. Kim von Post walked in like a bright bomb: straight back, eyes bright, hair a deliberate shade of electric blue that made the white walls look apologetic for being boring. Her glasses were big enough to be a dare. Today's T-shirt said "MATH: THE ONLY PLACE WHERE PEOPLE BUY 60 WATERMELONS AND NO ONE WONDERS WHY," and somehow it didn't look dumb on her.

"Good morning, brave ones," she said, placing a stack of worksheets on the counter and propping a piece of white paper against the board. "We've done Newton. We've done momentum. We've even survived my rant about units." A ripple of laughter; a couple of groans. "Today, we are going to nibble on something as large as time."

"That's what she said," someone muttered. The class snorted. Von Post let it pass, a pointed look with a small smile in one corner of her mouth, and lifted the paper.

"This," she said, "is spacetime. Don't panic. We're not doing calculus." She drew a line across the paper with a fat marker. "We like to imagine time as a line like this. Neat. Left to right. Past. Present. Future. One direction, like the band." A small laugh. "Your phones, " she flicked her eyes at the pockets where a dozen rectangles sulked, "your phones love this idea. Clocks love it. But the universe, as usual, is not a clock. Or a boy band."

Mercedes tipped her head back, already bored on purpose. Physics for her was the sound adults made when they needed you to be quiet.

Mandy sat up without meaning to. The word *time* flicked something in her ribs.

"We only ever live," von Post said, tapping the paper, "in the *present*. In *now*. Your memories are not time travel; they're stories your brain tells to keep you from exploding. The future isn't real yet, not here, not for you. 'Now' is it." She paused to let that be what it was. "But, and this is the fun bit, we can think about how 'now' is experienced. Every version of you, be it you at five years-old or you at seventy years-old goes through their own 'now.' We can think about the way different 'nows' might brush up against each other."

She pinched the paper at the short edges and bent it carefully until the ends almost touched. "If this paper is the universe, and you're here, and dinosaurs are here," she tapped two points, "there is no way in normal life to get from you to them. You can't march down the line to meet a T. rex. Dinosaurs are not your problem."

"Speak for yourself," a boy in front of Mandy murmured quietly to his friend. "My ex is a T. rex."

She held up the folded paper so the two points almost met. "But if the paper bends, if the *geometry* changes, suddenly two points that felt impossibly far are... neighbors. Not because you rewound anything. Not because you leapt backward. But because space and time were... persuaded to shake hands." She let the class look at the almost-touching dots. "You can't do this in your kitchen. Don't try. But this is one way physicists talk about things that are otherwise very slippery. Two 'nows' can get close enough to whisper."

Mercedes glanced sideways and caught Mandy watching too closely. She made a face that said *nerd* and then softened it, because it was also the face that said *I'll make fun of you so no one else can.*

"Now, before your brains revolt," von Post said, setting the paper down, "let's make this human. You all know what a lane change is. You're on a road, heading one way; you change lanes, still going forward, but you've committed to a different set of options, different exits, different traffic. You didn't reverse. You didn't hop into last Tuesday. You just... shifted."

"Because the other lane was faster," Mercedes stage-whispered.

"Or slower," Mandy said.

"Or had hotter drivers," someone added.

"Focus, hearts," von Post said, amused. "The metaphor is imperfect, don't email me, but it's helpful. If there are multiple possible 'lanes' of reality all existing as potentials, your choices in the present determine which lane you find yourself in later. Just 'now' and your steering wheel."

She let that sit and then added, like it was just another flavor at the ice-cream stand: "Also, cities have places where reality is... we'll call it *thin*. Old lines, tram lines, power corridors, even pre-modern pathways, we've built on top of them for a thousand years. Sometimes energy behaves a little weird there. Triangulations. Hotspots. It's not magic. It's just that systems can have weak spots. You know this from cracked phone screens."

The class liked that. At least five kids reflexively glanced down as if their screens could hear.

"Do we have 'thin' places here?" a girl in the front row asked, half challenge, half hope.

"We have *interesting* places," von Post said, flipping the marker cap on and off. "Triangles you can draw between old substations, bridges, hilltops. The city whispers in a grid if you're geeky enough to listen." She smiled to show that being geeky enough to listen was a compliment, not a prison. "But, before rumors start, we're not summoning ghosts. We're doing *physics.*"

Mercedes raised a finger, not quite a hand. "So, like, no time machines in the basement?"

"If there were," von Post said, "I would not be here teaching you. I would be in Crete in 1975, barefoot, and you would all fail this course." Laughter. "No machines. No past travel. Just an insistence on the preciousness of *now*, and curiosity about how *nows* can brush."

Brush, Mandy thought. The word made sense. The first time the red numbers had shown up, it had felt like the room brushing against another room. Not a collision. A nudge.

Von Post moved on to a quick clip of an animation, folded surfaces, points kissing in space, a visual metaphor that made the class collectively go "oooh" and then "ugh" when the equations slid up underneath. "Don't panic," she said again. "The math can wait. Just keep the picture. Paper that can bend. Nows that can whisper. Lane changes. Again, science does not call this time-travel, there is no such thing, okay? It's more like... parallel realities."

While the class copied a diagram she drew, Mercedes bent her head toward Mandy. "If she grades on how cool your hair is, we're all failing."

"Good thing she grades on units," Mandy murmured.

Mercedes rolled her eyes and mouthed, *nerd.* Mandy bit back a smile.

When the bell gave its bored buzz, chairs scraped back and bodies funneled toward the door in the usual good-natured stampede. Von Post raised her voice just enough to ride over the scrape. "Homework: write one paragraph about a moment that made you want to change your 'lane.' Made you want to experience a different 'now.' Half a page is fine." A few groans, a few laughs. "And, this is optional, but if you ever feel like time goes... strange?" She shrugged like it was nothing. "Write it down. What time it was, where you were. Phones are unreliable; your brains are worse. Logs help."

The sentence landed in Mandy like a pin. She kept her face neutral, lab calm. *Optional.* She could ignore it. She could not.

Most of the class poured out. Mandy pretended to adjust her backpack until the cluster around von Post thinned, then stepped closer to the desk. Up close, the blue in the teacher's hair was even more deliberate, streaks of lighter electric threaded through darker ocean, a storm caught too soon to rain. Her eyes were the kind that saw things and didn't announce it.

"Ms. von Post?" Mandy said, aware that her voice wanted to be too soft and making it normal. "The... lane-change thing. It makes sense. I think."

"Good," von Post said. "Sense is all we have. And sometimes not even that."

Mandy surprised herself by smiling. "I like the paper thing. Dinosaurs walking now, right there, but not for us."

"That's my favorite too," von Post said. "We carry a lot of ghosts, dinosaur ghosts, city ghosts, our own ghosts. The trick is not letting them drive." She tilted her head. "You looked alert today."

"Caffeine," Mandy lied.

"Caffeine does not make people listen," von Post said, amused. "Just shake." She capped the marker and set it down, assessing Mandy for a few seconds as if she were contemplating whether to say what she wanted to. "Look Mandy, I know you are going through a hard time. If you ever want to share the load of extra problems, I am here for you. If you ever feel weird, keep the log. Journal it out. No pressure, but if science has taught us something, it's that data makes the universe look less rude."

"Data," Mandy repeated, as if the syllables themselves could be armor. "Right."

"Go eat something that isn't... bland cafeteria food,'" von Post said, waving her toward the door. "Your brains need color."

Mercedes had waited, because she always did, leaning against the hall radiator like it belonged to her. "Tell me you were not asking for extra homework," she said, as they fell into step.

"I was asking for the secret to not falling asleep," Mandy said.

"Which is: don't come to physics," Mercedes said, pleased with herself. She pulled her hood up, then down, indecisive. "Also, the cafeteria is actually doing puke soup. I checked."

"You manifested it," Mandy said.

"Obviously," Mercedes said. "We're going downtown. I'm not eating anything that looks even remotely off."

Mandy agreed. They turned the corner with the tide of other students and let the hall decide their speed. Someone had stuck a sticker of a cartoon cat to the fire extinguisher sign. Someone else had drawn a speech bubble for the cat that said *help*.

"Hey, question," Mercedes said, talking fast the way she did when she didn't want to hear the answer. "If we do the micro-visit after school, you're not going to... you know... vanish on me, right? Into a book or a coma?"

"I haven't vanished on you once," Mandy said, more defensive than she meant. "I'm here." She spread her hands. "Fully present. Now."

"Ugh, don't say 'now' like Ms. Von Post," Mercedes said. "I think I have become allergic to that word." She gagged before veering back into cafeteria commentary. "Do you remember when they served that rice that squeaked? Rice should not squeak. Food should not speak unless it's saying, 'hello, I am bread.'"

"Bread is fluent," Mandy said, grateful for the way Mercedes could deploy ridiculousness like a blanket. "Bread took two years of Swedish and is doing very well."

They were still riffing on bread's academic career when the corridor did the thing again.

It was small. It was not the kind of thing a person could point to and say, *See.* The lights didn't go out; they *stuttered*, a quick strobe like a camera flash from three rooms away. The hum that lived in the fluorescent tubes shifted half a note lower and then back. Mandy's hearing went weird, like when you're on a plane and your ears don't pop, a pressure you can taste. Her skin felt half a size too tight. It was the sensation of an elevator slipping one inch before it found the floor.

Did you hear
what I said?

Then it was over. The light was light again. The hum was itself. The hallway filled with the noise of people being people.

"...did you hear what I said?" Mercedes was mid-yap and mid-gesture, hand in the air as if her thought had been a plane that needed landing clearance. Her face proposed a joke and then reconsidered. "Yo, you okay?"

Mandy's phone was in her hand that she didn't remember raising. The screen showed nothing red. Just **11:25** while she could have sworn it was **11:22** just a second ago.

Her throat went tight. She forced breath in through her nose like the gym teacher had taught them once. *Head forward. Breathe steady.* It wasn't blood this time. It was a wave. If she tried to stand against it, she'd get knocked over. If she let it pass she might still be standing when it was gone.

"Bathroom," she said, not loud, and Mercedes, bless her, curse her, did not ask another question. She just pivoted like a fish and cut through the current toward the girls' room, dragging Mandy by a sleeve because that was simpler than any sentence.

Inside, the light existed in a different way, white, flat, certain. The stalls were mostly closed. Someone was crying quietly in the last one. Someone else was telling a story into their phone in the mirror and examining their eyebrows for lies. The air smelled like hand soap and a lemon cleaner that did nothing except announce that someone had tried. The sound of a toilet flushing came from somewhere else, like in a dream.

Mercedes pushed the middle stall door open with two knuckles and steered Mandy in. "Breathe," she said, as if Mandy had forgotten the instructions for living in a body. She didn't add *I've got you*, but it was in the way she stood in the doorway like a guard dog.

Mandy locked the latch and sat. She put her elbows on her knees and her hands over her face, and she listened to the things that were not panic: shoes scuffing, water running, someone exclaiming about a text from a crush with happiness.

Her phone lay cold in her palm. She stared at the black glass and wanted to throw it and wanted to press it to her sternum like a talisman. She did neither. She unlocked it and opened the Notes app without looking at her messages.

Optional, von Post had said. Writing it down helps.

Mandy typed:

11:25 – corridor between physics + cafeteria. Lights strobe. Hearing… *warbly?* Felt like pressure. Felt like time jumped? But could have lost track of it. (11:**22** → **11:25).** No red numbers. No Dad/type man.

She stared at the words. They didn't look like hers. They looked like something a person wrote to pretend they were calm. She added:

(don't panic.)

"All good?" Mercedes asked from the crack in the door. She'd dropped her voice into the register she only used late at night and very early in the morning.

"Yeah," Mandy lied, then changed it. "I'm... okay. Just got overwhelmed." She stood, flushed, checked herself in the little metal mirror inside the stall, no blood, just a face that needed a nap, and unlocked the door.

Mercedes stepped back to give her space to pass and then fell into step beside her again like a wing. They washed their hands longer than necessary. The soap was too perfumed. The water was too cold. It was all fine.

On the way out, Mandy paused at the paper towel bin and tossed the wad like a free throw. It arced, hit the rim, and fell in.

"Lunch," Mercedes decreed, as if the act of naming it could make it edible. "We walk past puke soup like queens. We glide. We breathe through our mouths. We plan our escape. We do not faint."

"I'm not going to faint," Mandy said, and heard how much she wanted that to be true. "I'm... fine."

"Fine," Mercedes echoed, and then, lighter: "Also, I am manifesting a cinnamon bun that is not dry. If I stare at the display like I love it, it will love me back."

"That's not how buns work," Mandy said.

"Buns are sentient," Mercedes said. "That's physics."

"Not *our* physics," Mandy said, and then wished she hadn't said *our* like she had ownership of a class or a teacher or a set of pretty ideas that could explain the unexplainable. She didn't.

Mandy kept her phone at her side like a sleeping animal and didn't check it again until they were at the cafeteria entrance and the smell of soup hit them like a wall.

"Fuck," Mercedes whispered, hand to her heart.

"Lane change," Mandy whispered back, and wasn't sure if she meant lunch plans or something else entirely.

CHAPTER 4

They'd been in the line outside Bianca's boutique long enough for Mandy's toes to go from numb to philosophical. March did that in Stockholm: pretended to be spring from behind glass, then walked past you outdoors with a bucket of cold water and no apology. The girls had dressed like they were going to be seen: eyeliner straight enough to pass inspection, hair that had opinions, coats they'd borrowed from themselves to pretend they were warmer than they were.

"What can we *not* do for Bianca?" Mercedes said through chattering teeth, bouncing in place. "Sacrifice our bodies to frostbite? Done. Sell a kidney? Preferably someone else's? Done."

"I have to pee," Mandy said, folding forward to put pressure on the ache that had been gnawing since morning. The cold made it feel like glass in her stomach. "Like, *now*."

"Hold it," Mercedes said, eyes shining. "We are so close to the kingdom. Look. Look!" She grabbed Mandy's sleeve and pointed, hopping once like a little kid even though she would die if anyone called her that.

A white car the shape of a perfect thought eased to the curb and paused in the way expensive cars did, as if the world arranged itself around them. The doors opened and **Bianca** climbed out, small and spectacular, her entourage arranging itself into weather around her. She wore a coat that believed in itself. The cameras fluttered like sparrows.

"Bianca!" Mercedes and a half-dozen other girls sang, hands up as if that could make the sound skip the queue.

Bianca did what she did: smiled at the middle distance, waved, skated across the few meters from car to door without seeing anyone in particular. That was part of the magic, no one could be disappointed if no one had been promised. Mandy's lips had gone bluish; she pressed them together and thought: *Not now. Not now.* She remembered the Denmark trip in fifth grade where the teacher had said bodily needs were like the tides:

Bianca's

"They pass if you pretend they aren't there." She'd hated that teacher.

Mercedes cupped her hands to her mouth. "She looked at us," she declared after a beat. "She *did*. I am choosing to believe."

"I support your choices," Mandy said, because it cost nothing and because the believing warmed them a little.

The doors opened and the line funneled into the boutique's bright air. The light inside had a temperature of its own; the space smelled like eucalyptus and a thousand krone candles that said things like *Focus* and *Lux*. People moved like they were in a video, all straight backs and turning heads and clothes that didn't pucker anywhere. A small stage had been built near the back, and Bianca, already miked, stood on it and lifted an elegant hand.

"Hi, everyone," she sang in a voice that sounded both practiced and intimate. "Welcome to my boutique." The crowd answered with the kind of cheer that was air and hunger. "Don't forget to get my advent calendar, today only 1,995 kronor." She smiled exactly the right amount and pointed to a display like a magician doing a reveal. People moved toward it as if compelled by physics.

Mandy slid sideways out of the current and parked near a mirrored pillar to watch people watch themselves. She had brought a pen, Olle's gift her last birthday, just in case. She tucked it deeper into her pocket, suddenly embarrassed by the idea of her and a marker hovering near Bianca's perfect sleeve. Autographs belonged to a different century anyway.

Mercedes moved in a pattern only she knew: step, pause, glance, step. It looked like idle browsing. It was not. Her hand slid along a row of lip gloss testers with absent-minded care and then, when no one looked directly at her, her palm closed and her sleeve swallowed a little tube the color of pomegranate. Mandy didn't gasp; she was too busy *distracting*, stepping into the path of a store assistant with a harmless question—"Hi, what's the undertone on that nude?"—and a smile that read as customer, not security problem.

"The undertone?" the assistant repeated, excited to explain. "It's neutral-warm. Very wearable."

"Of course it is," Mandy said, nodding like a person with a budget. "Thanks."

They met by the mirror again, faces good in the light, hearts doing tiny tap routines behind their ribs.

"It's like a museum," Mercedes whispered, giddy. "Except the paintings are clothes."

"And security guards," Mandy said, glancing at the pair of men pretending to be potted plants. The lip gloss in Mercedes's sleeve felt like a living thing between them. Shoplifting always did: small, dumb, thrilling, a way to tell the world you could take up space even if you couldn't pay rent in it.

They glided toward the window, because even queens needed air. The glass was a performance stage; the street outside watched them watching it.

That was when they saw him.

Bilal moved through the blanched light with that tilt some boys had, the one that said nothing could surprise them because they'd learned everything the hard way already. He was eighteen the way a burned-out lightbulb is eighteen: used too often, taken out and shaken, screwed back in. He kept his eyes on his phone, scrolling a clip where a masked man spun two pistols while banknotes fell like a joke about weather. The screen made a small oasis of moving color in the gray.

Mandy's mouth went dry. Everyone knew Bilal. He belonged to the neighborhood like graffiti did: loud, sometimes beautiful, often a problem. He and his crew had a way of being in a place that made other people decide to be somewhere else. He was a bad idea with good bone structure. Boys like that taught whole schools a lesson for free: *do not look too long.*

Mercedes looked too long. When Bilal's gaze lifted, like a person remembering that streets have horizons, it snagged on hers through the boutique glass. For a breath there was no glass at all. There was a girl with flushed cheeks and a mouth already halfway into a smile she couldn't afford, and there was a boy whose eyes, sad, tired, did not match the clip on his screen.

He pressed a heart on the clip without looking down. Mercedes blushed so fast it felt like a small sunburn. She fumbled the top she'd been pretending to consider and put it back wrong.

"Don't," Mandy said, too late for anything but for this: a small, protective edge to her voice.

"I'm not doing anything," Mercedes said, though her whole face was doing something. "He looked at me."

"He looks at everyone," Mandy said. "It's his hobby."

"He looked at me," Mercedes repeated, like a proof you couldn't argue with. The glass reflected three versions of her face, and all of them were happy to be argued with if it meant more attention.

They followed the current out. The door breathed them into the cold. The city resumed its old voice. Bilal had already turned the corner, as if he were a coin trick.

"Don't," Mandy said again, because she needed to have said it once, even if no one listened. "He's not—"

"I know what he is," Mercedes said.

Mandy believed her. That was the trouble.

∧∨∧

By the time Mandy got home, the house had exhaled and gone still. The lasagna her mother had made and left covered on the stove had congealed into comfort if you squinted. Mandy kicked her shoes off on the mat, ignored the plate, and went straight to her room. Her head throbbed; her stomach had found a new rhythm. She unbuttoned her jeans with one hand and fell onto the bed with the other, phone cupped in her palm like a none-too-gentle pet.

She put the phone down, closed her eyes, and the room thickened, the way rooms did sometimes right before you fell asleep or right before the lights went out in a storm. The corner near the wardrobe pushed closer. A man stood there like a sentence that had been cut out of a story and pasted back in. He wore the jacket he always wore when he was alive, and it made no sense that fabric could be faithful to a memory.

He didn't speak. Like always. He lifted a hand and **pointed** at the phone.

Mandy's eyes snapped open. Her heart behaved like she had run stairs. On the phone: **57:12:59**, red, too saturated, rolls down to **57:12:58**. The digits were wrong on this screen in the same way a wolf would be wrong in a kindergarten classroom: it didn't matter that it was quiet; its presence made the air different.

She blinked to clear the grit. When her lids slid up, the corner was a corner again, a wardrobe that needed dusting. The phone showed **19:04**, and Mercedes's name glowed with a new message as if nothing unusual had happened to bring it to her.

Mandy licked her lips. They were dry. She pressed two fingers under her nose and found a smear of red that wasn't dramatic enough to be frightening and wasn't small enough to ignore. In her chest was the hollow that came after a scare was over and hadn't taught you anything except how to be scared.

She lay there for a minute because lying there was easier than being a person. From the kitchen, the radio was still set to the station that believed mornings belonged to men arguing. Someone said the word *explosion* like it was a vocabulary word and not an event.

Her phone buzzed again. She turned it face up.

Merce: tell me u saw him
Merce: like saw-saw
Merce: i can't breathe
Merce: should i dm
Merce: i dm'd
Merce: i hate me lol
Merce: he added me back

Mandy typed and erased and typed again.

Mandy: careful

She watched the typing bubble appear and disappear like a heartbeat in blue.

Merce: i am always careful
Merce: i am the MOST careful
Merce: ok not really
Merce: but this is... idk
Merce: it's not nothing

Mandy's thumbs hovered.

Mandy: he's not a movie
Mandy: he's a fire

It was both too dramatic and not dramatic enough to be true. Mercedes hearted it anyway.

Merce: ok poet
Merce: ok mandy "metaphor" mild
Merce: brb

The thread went quiet. Mandy lay still and tried to feel normal. After a minute, she swung her legs off the bed and sat up too fast. The room did not spin; it receded, just slightly, the way a receding wave made you sway and think about balance. She breathed until the hum in her ears dialed itself down.

She washed her face. She ate a square of lasagna she couldn't taste. She opened her homework and looked at the words and decided to be kind to herself and close the book again. She put the pen Olle had given her in the pencil cup where it belonged. She didn't open the chat. She didn't think about the red numbers. She did not, absolutely did not, think about the way the man had pointed, like a conductor giving a downbeat.

By the time midnight rolled out, she slept, or something that pretended well enough to count.

∧∨∧

Morning came like a negotiation. Mandy's hair had decided to become a nest in the night and refused to be anything else. She plugged in the straightener and loved it the way a person loved a friend who always showed up. Halfway through coaxing the worst of it into obedience, a bang on the window made her jump so badly the flat iron clanged to the floor.

"Fucking hell—fuck!" she hissed, lunging to make sure the cord hadn't melted carpet. She popped the latch on the window and shoved it up.

Mercedes was outside, breath fogging a circle on the glass, eyes enormous with the kind of excitement that made her look fourteen and forty at the same time. She rubbed a clear patch and pressed her mouth to it. "Hey! Open up!" her voice came through the pane, muffled and delighted and not quite in the right key.

MANDY

Mandy hauled her in by the wrist, which would have been smooth if Mercedes's boot hadn't caught the lip of the sill and knocked a plant pot onto the floor. It was metal, thank god, but soil did the thing soil did: announced its presence.

"Aaah! You Hippo!" Mandy said automatically. "Can you be more clumsy?"

"Fuck," Mercedes panted, hands on her knees for one second before remembering why she'd come. "Okay. Okay. Listen." She sucked air like she'd been running. "Bilal."

"Bilal what?" Mandy said, picking up the straightener and pretending her hands weren't shaking.

"Bilal wants to meet." The words came out in a rush and landed like a glass on a table. "Like, me. Me-me. After school. Downtown." The last word stretched into a shape that held both romance and danger the way teenage brains did, one bleeding into the other, a cocktail with too much sugar.

Mandy stared at her, then at the little renovations the plant had made to her floor, then back. "Is that a good idea?" she said, aiming for neutral and landing somewhere near big sister.

"I know who he hangs with," Mercedes said fast, anticipatory, the way you argue before someone says no. "I'm not an idiot. But he's... he's nice." She heard herself and made a face. "Or whatever the boy version of nice is when you're tired and a little scary."

"You sure you're not just... into the movie in your head?" Mandy asked, gentler. "The whole 'danger but make it beautiful' thing?"

"I'm not stupid," Mercedes said, but not like she wanted to fight. She looked at the corner of the floor where the plant had spilled and then at Mandy. "You don't want this for me, do you? Don't tell me you are jealous!"

"That's not fair," Mandy said, and meant it. "I want you to get good things. I just... want them to not stab you."

Mercedes fell quiet, a low rise of embarrassment on her face. "Right," she said, sighing. "But he seems nice, I... I like him. I want to go."

"Okay," Mandy said, then sighed. "But also: I'm coming with you. If you're going, I'm going. Not because I want to micro-control you, but because I'm not letting you be out there with him alone. Not until we can trust him."

"Okay," Mercedes said softly, relief and thrill shaking hands in her voice. "We leave before last class. He said downtown." She leaned in, forehead to forehead for a second, like a pact. "We'll be subtle."

"Subtle," Mandy said dryly. "Like a whisper."

"Like a thought," Mercedes said, grinning. She wiggled back through the window and promptly elbowed the other plant pot. It thunked to the floor and coughed up a little more dirt.

There was a knock at the bedroom door. "Are you okay in there, darling?" Mandy's mom called.

"Hippo," Mandy whispered toward the window, a fond insult that had become a pet name. Mercedes mouthed sorry and dropped onto the flowerbed below like the fall was two stories and not one meter. "I'll see you out the door in like five minutes."

The knock came again, closer to concern. Mandy's fuse, already short, sparked. "Oh my god," she shouted, too loud, at the universe and at the door. "Can everyone leave me alone?!"

"Don't swear," her mother said mildly from the other side, which only made Mandy feel worse. "And don't leave without breakfast!"

Mandy locked eyes with her own reflection: hair half-straight, mouth too sharp, eyes too awake. She took the straightener back to the part of her hair that resisted and pressed until it gave in. She wasn't sure if she wanted the day to hurry or stall.

Her phone buzzed on the desk. Mercedes: 2pm, fountain by the old cinema. u and me. don't die before that pls. A second later: jk i'd fight god.

Mandy typed back: i know you would and tucked the phone into her pocket like it could keep time honest.

Somewhere out past the glass, the city didn't make sense, and Mandy didn't know where to start piecing her thoughts together. She knew only that when her father appeared, he pointed at the phone, and when Mercedes laughed, the air got warmer, and when clocks jumped, she felt the world tilt. She would go to the fountain. She would go with her best friend. She would keep a hand on her present and try not to look for weird numbers unless they came looking for her.

CHAPTER 5

They were early by twenty minutes because Mercedes couldn't sit still in class and because Mandy refused to let her go alone. The "downtown" meet point turned out not to be glamorous at all—just the lee of a shuttered café by the tram loop where pigeons made a living on dropped fries and the wind came around the corner with opinions.

Mercedes checked her phone every forty seconds without looking like she was checking. She did it like a tic, like a person brushing hair out of their eyes that wasn't there. Mandy leaned on the railing that kept people from falling into the tracks and tried to let the city's regular noises wash away the other kind that were living in her head lately—warble, strobe, the feel of rooms taking a breath.

"Stop looking," Mandy said finally, gentle.

"I'm not looking," Mercedes lied. She switched hands and looked again. "He said after last period. This is after."

"It's still after in ten minutes," Mandy said. "After is big."

Mercedes made a sound that was not a word. A tram hummed in, brake squeal high and thin, then sighed away again, taking the easier stories with it. The sky was the color of a coin someone had held too long.

At five past, Mercedes laughed. It was the kind of laugh you used when you didn't want to use your other choices. "He's late. Classic."

"At fifteen past," Mandy said, "we get cinnamon buns and we pretend this was a micro-visit to the tram."

"At twenty past we text him 'lol sorry we left,'" Mercedes said. She tried to make it a joke and it didn't hurt less.

By half-an hour past, both of them were cold through their jeans. Mercedes held her phone like it was hot and stared at the blank screen anyway, willing it to shiver. It didn't. She put it away. She took it out.

"He's not coming," Mandy said softly, because someone needed to say it out loud so reality could hear and sit down.

Mercedes's mouth did the I'm-okay tilt. "He's coming," she said, and then, because the tilt hurt to hold, "He's busy. He's... you know. Busy."

Mandy nodded as if this was a thing that could be true. She hooked her hand through Mercedes's elbow. "Buns," she said, and didn't wait for agreement.

The bakery smelled like safety and yeast. They stood at the counter and stared at the trays as if they were maps, then ended up at a window table with napkins that were too small and sugar on their fingers that didn't feel like a victory. Mercedes checked her phone under the table. Once. Twice. The third time she didn't bother hiding it.

"Maybe his battery died," Mandy offered, the way you offer a blanket you know is too thin but warm anyway.

Mercedes nodded so fast her ponytail swung. "Or he got pulled into something. Like, actual real, shady... things. Not... us."

"Or he changed his mind," Mandy said, because truth sometimes got the bleeding over with faster. She braced herself for the flinch.

The flinch came and went. Mercedes took a shaky breath that made her rib cage flutter. "I hate that," she said, eyes on the glass where pedestrians walked through the reflection of their faces. "I hate that he could just... decide. Like I'm a playlist he can skip."

"You're not a playlist," Mandy said. "You're a whole... album." She winced. "That sounds worse."

"It does," Mercedes said, and snorted a laugh around it anyway. Then the laugh toppled into the space beside it and wasn't one. "Why doesn't he—" She put both hands over her face and spoke into them. "Why wouldn't he want me back?"

Mandy's throat did the wrong thing. She had no good answer that wasn't spendy with truth. "He doesn't know you yet," she said instead. "He knows a version of you. From stranger glances. From... vibes. He doesn't get to know you from that."

"But I like him," Mercedes said, which was both a confession and a curse. "I like him and it makes me feel like I'm made of... pink steam. Like I could float out of my own skin."

"You're allowed to like him," Mandy said. She reached across the table and touched Mercedes's knuckles. "It doesn't make him worth it."

Mercedes looked at their hands as if they were someone else's. "I hate him," she said, and then, with the stubbornness that had kept her alive in rooms that didn't want her, "I also don't."

They went home in the grey that happened between afternoon and evening when the sky hadn't decided what story to tell. Mercedes peeled off at her tram and didn't look back, probably because looking back would hurt and also because she understood that if she did, Mandy would have to wave.

∧∨∧

"Lasagna," Mandy's mother announced, like a weather forecast she hoped would be well-received. The kitchen was warm and bright in that cozy, slightly desperate way that came from trying. The radio had been mercifully turned off. The table had been wiped too hard.

"I'm not—" Mandy started, defaulting to the sharp. The look on her mother's face stopped her, a small collapse around the eyes that said *please meet me halfway.* "Okay," she amended, and put her bag down on the chair that always caught straps.

"Mercedes coming?" her mother asked, without looking up from the pan she was carving into squares.

"Later," Mandy said, which wasn't a plan but a hope that felt like one. Instead, it was an hour later and Mercedes was in Mandy's room on her stomach on the rug, scrolling with a motion that wasn't reading. The blue from her phone made her look a little drowned. A slice of lasagna cooled next to her and went uneaten.

Mandy sat cross-legged on the bed and picked at a loose thread in the blanket, winding it around her finger and then unwinding it as if she could use it like a rosary to count their way toward feeling less dumb.

"He posted a story," Mercedes said finally, into the quiet. "Skating. With some guys. Like... not even pretending to be busy."

Mandy felt the pinch under her ribs again, that tight little organ that lived between jealousy and fear. "Maybe it was old," she tried. "People post old."

"He tagged today," Mercedes said, flat.

"Oh," Mandy said. It was such a small word for something so sharp.

"Do you think he thought I was... kidding?" Mercedes asked. "Like, that he didn't believe me. That he thought I wouldn't come. Or that I was clowning him."

"He knows you came," Mandy said. "He's got eyes everywhere." The bitterness surprised her. She turned it down. "We already know that."

"You think I scared him with my eagerness?" Mercedes said, then shook her head because that was laughable. "No. He doesn't scare."

"Mmm," Mandy said, noncommittal, which in their language meant he definitely doesn't.

Her mom knocked on the door and then cracked it without waiting. "Oh hey, Mercedes." She brightened that tiny bit; it was honest. "There you are. I made the salad with the good cucumbers." She held two plates like offerings. "I made extra," she said, as if extra were a spell.

"Thank you," Mercedes said, flipping onto her back and propping herself on her elbows. "You're an angel."

Mandy's mother set the plates on the desk and pretended she didn't see the dampness at the corners of Mercedes's eyes. She was very good at pretending not to see. "I'm watching that gardening show, so I'll be... not here." She squeezed the door handle in an air-hug and closed them in again.

They ate because sometimes chewing was a thing to do with your body when feelings didn't want to be told to sit. The lasagna tasted like cheese and kindness. Mandy found herself hungrier than she thought and cleaned her plate without ceremony.

"I hate him," Mercedes said again, a little meatier now the edge of hunger had been sawed off. "I hate that he can... do that. That he can just not show and then go skate and laugh and be..." She waved her fork as if it could draw the shape she meant.

"Boys are allowed," Mandy said, and wished it wasn't true.

"Allowed to be princes... or more like, gangsters," Mercedes said, biting the last word. "And we're... extras."

"We are main characters," Mandy said, trying to make it a fact.

Mercedes pointed her fork like a judge. "Say it again, but slower, and with confetti."

"Main characters," Mandy said, and smiled because they both needed to.

They watched something stupid on Mandy's laptop because stupid was the Swiss Army knife of evenings. They laughed, even, for real. When Mercedes finally left, she hugged Mandy hard at the door like a brace and said, "Tomorrow, we do something that makes me forget his name."

"Tomorrow," Mandy echoed, and then they both looked at the clock like it was a person and rolled their eyes at it and the meanness of time.

ᴧⱴᴧ

Tomorrow was not interested in being kind.

They did not set out to steal. That was the dangerous part: how often it happened by drift. They were in the mall because heat and because the cinnamon bun stall had done a fresh batch that shone. They pulled each other from store to store like bright fish following a light. In the third shop, the one with the stupidly helpful clerks, Mercedes found a compact that made her skin look like it lived somewhere closer to the equator and held it just a second too long.

"I can't," she said, sighing in a tone that begged a fight.

"Then don't," Mandy said, meaning it.

Mercedes tucked the compact into the crook of her wrist and Mandy did not say put it back because the world had narrowed to the size of that clerk's eyes: chatty, bored, not bored enough. The security antenna at the door hummed in the way Mandy could feel in her teeth, and suddenly there were two possible futures pressed up against each other—either they got caught or they didn't.

"Let's go," Mercedes said, the word shaped like a dare. She breezed toward the door like a person who had paid for things all her life and still liked doing it.

The alarm hiccuped. It wasn't the full siren; it was a wounded little beep, like a toy about to die. The clerk glanced up. The security guard two stores over looked down at his own phone. No one moved, and that was their moment, and they took it without style. They walked too fast. Then they ran.

"Subtle," Mandy hissed, and then laughed out loud because they had already blown subtle apart.

They cut left past the plant shop and right through the cheap shoes. Once outside, the air hit them like truth. Mercedes's laugh turned giddy with survival. "We're gods," she said, breathless.

"Don't," Mandy said, breathless, and then, because the universe loved a follow-up, her phone buzzed in her pocket. She pulled it out. The message was not from any god. It was from a number she didn't know that somehow knew her and Mercedes as if the names had always been connected.

Unknown: Two little birds just flew without paying.
Unknown: Industrial road. Deserted alley. Fifteen minutes.
Unknown: Come or it gets expensive.

Mercedes read over her shoulder and all the happiness dropped out of her face like a trapdoor. "Shit."

Mandy's stomach tightened so hard it folded her forward, a pain she could call cramps if she wanted to be kind to herself. She didn't need to answer the text. She didn't need to type anything at all. Her phone vibrated again.

Unknown: Don't text back. Just come.

"Who is—" Mercedes started, then cut herself off because the answer stood up in her skin and wouldn't let the sentence finish.

They went because that was what people did when power texted. They went because don't text back was the kind of sentence you obeyed if you wanted to be alive tomorrow. They went because, together, you could pretend you were making a choice.

The industrial road was the kind that could be anywhere, gray buildings with corrugated ribs, a smell of oil that got into the mouth, the occasional dignified stomp of a truck minding its own business. The dark dusty alley loomed like the idea of giants. Gravel betrayed their footsteps and made it sound like they were telling on themselves. Mandy tasted metal.

He was there. He leaned on a matte black bike that looked like a movie prop and did delicate things with his phone as if the phone had offended him and only exact taps would be accepted.

"Hi," Mercedes said, which was ridiculous and also brave.

Bilal looked up. He wasn't smiling, his eyes were a different level of darkness than she had ever witnessed earlier. His face was one you could draw with a ruler, clean angles, and something soft at the mouth that did not belong in this alley. If Mandy hadn't already known his name, the way he occupied the space would have told her.

"You didn't show," Mercedes blurted, and then flinched like she'd heard herself from outside her body.

Bilal's eyebrow moved up a degree. "You say that like I owe you."

"I—" Mercedes started, and stopped. "We—"

He cut the word in half with a small hand gesture. It was not rude. It was… efficient. He flicked his eyes to the bag swinging at Mercedes's wrist, the one with the compact nested like guilt inside. "You're funny girls," he said. His tone was almost affectionate, which made it worse. "Funny to run that in there."

"We didn't—" Mandy started, loyal by reflex.

He didn't look at her. "You stole on my turf." Still almost gentle. Like he was explaining a rule to a child who had not read the game's manual. "You owe."

Mercedes tried to laugh but her throat refused. "Owe what?"

"Fifty thousand," Bilal said, plain as a price tag. "Or you do a bag for me. A drop. No questions. No selfies. You take it. You leave it. You walk away. You don't look back."

"That's—" Mandy found her voice and lost it on the shape of the number. "We're—We can't—"

"You can," Bilal said mildly, and then let the mildness slide away to show the steel under it. "Or I will show your mama where you were. She's alone a lot, right?" He cocked his head, and the angle made him look suddenly very young and very tired. "Hard to keep a door safe when you sleep. Hard to keep a face pretty when it meets a wall."

The words rearranged Mercedes's posture like hands. She did not crumple because she did not do that, but it was a near thing. "Don't," she said. Just that. Just, *please don't hurt my mom.*

"Then don't be stupid," he said, with an almost bored patience that made Mandy angrier than a shout would have. "You girls are ghosts. You look clean, you pass through cameras, people skip you when they watch the tape. My perfect little ghost couriers... that's a real thing, you know? I didn't invent it though. I'm just offering you employment."

"Employment," Mandy said, and had to bite down on the laugh that wanted to be a scream. "Do we get a W-2, or..."

His gaze came to her then, finally, and it was like standing under a streetlight that went out and then decided to turn back on. "You have a mouth," he said. There was no threat in it, not exactly. "Use it to say yes."

Mandy shut her mouth.

Bilal turned back to Mercedes, which was where he had been looking all along, even when his eyes had been on his phone. "It's not personal," he said, and it sounded like a lie he told himself so he could sleep. "You do this, and I don't remember your names."

Mercedes searched his face for an angle that wasn't a trap. She found one, or told herself she did. "Okay," she said, as if a contract existed and he had just signed it. "We do it, and we're done."

He nodded, approving her for recognizing the terms he'd always planned. "This week," he said. "Pickup at the big silos. I'll send you the pin and all details. Don't overthink it... you will know the drill. It's just in and out." His mouth curved, not unkindly. "Dress like you're going to Bianca."

Something in Mandy's chest clicked. "If... we end up saying no?" she asked, because questions were the only weapon she had left that didn't look like a weapon.

He didn't answer. He looked at Mercedes again and out of nowhere, like a trick, he softened, just a fraction, enough for a human to step through. "I don't want to hurt your people," he said, and the *I* in that sentence was true. "Don't make me have to want to hurt you."

"Why us?" Mercedes asked, voice very small now that the big ones had been used up. "There are so many—"

"Because you're here," he said, shrugging one shoulder. "Because I need this done, and you need me not to be a problem."

The math was terrible and clean. Mandy hated how it balanced.

He slid his phone into his pocket and swung his leg over the bike like a door swinging to. For a second the boy he hadn't had time to be leaked through the cracks, the kid who played football in the parking lot and took too long a shower after and got in trouble for making the water cold for his brother. Then the engine coughed to life and the boy sealed back up and the man who stayed looked like nothing but forward.

"This week," he said again, and rolled away without waiting for their answer because he already had it.

They stood in the gritty air and let the shape of the encounter harden around them.

"Don't cry," Mandy said, even though Mercedes was not crying. It came out like a prayer.

"I'm not," Mercedes said, and she wasn't. She was doing that other thing—the stiffening. The turning to wood so you could float. "We'll do it. And then we'll be done."

"We'll get help," Mandy said. The sentence sounded like a plan if she didn't examine it.

"From who?" Mercedes asked, and it wasn't rhetorical. "The school? Your mom? The police?" Her laugh was short and had no humor in it. "No one is coming, Mand. This is the gang we are talking about."

Mandy wanted to say something comforting. Instead she said, "We're not alone," which was true in a way that felt both cosmic and stupid in this alley.

Mercedes nodded as if that counted. "You'll be with me," she said. "You won't... not be."

"Yeah," Mandy said quietly. On the way home, they didn't talk. They walked fast, like people late to a thing that would forgive them anyway.

At a crosswalk, the tick-tick stuttered and then resumed. Mercedes flicked her eyes to the signal like she could threaten it into behaving. Mandy watched the numbers on the opposite countdown flash and felt, for a second, an overlay of red under them... 00:10... 00:09... that made her stomach pitch like a boat. She blinked, then overlay was gone.

"See you tomorrow then," Mercedes said, when they split at the curb outside Mandy's building.

"Tomorrow," Mandy said. She had meant *good night* and said *good luck* by mistake. Which, in this city, were sometimes the same.

CHAPTER 6

Mercedes wasn't talking.

That was the first sign.

Normally, even when she said she wasn't talking, she was. Her mouth would keep moving because silence made her itchy. She'd fill space with anything, complaints about cafeteria food, a forensic analysis of which ninth grader was trying too hard with eyeliner, whether bread had feelings. She'd spin little dramas out of boring air just so the air wouldn't feel heavy.

Now, there was just heavy.

They were in Mandy's room, the same room where they had laughed about love and lasagna the night before, except there was no laughing now. Mercedes lay flat on her back on Mandy's bed, one arm thrown over her eyes, the other limp at her side like her battery had finally died. Her shoes were still on. That was new too. Mercedes was the type to kick her shoes off the second she crossed the threshold of somewhere she felt safe, usually complaining dramatically about circulation and "these boots are oppression." Now the boots were still on, heels leaving faint dirt half-moons on the comforter. She didn't care.

Mandy was on the floor, cross-legged, spine against the side of the bed, close enough that Mercedes's elbow almost touched her hair. She kept glancing at Mercedes's face, even though most of it was hidden. She kept not asking Are you okay? because she already knew the answer and also because that question was insulting when someone had just been told their mom could get her face kicked in as collateral.

It wasn't a boy problem. That was what made it worse. If it were just heartbreak, Mandy could have handled it. She could've said: he's trash, we've seen hotter, I will set him on metaphorical fire for you, pick a revenge outfit. They'd done versions of that for each other a thousand times, in miniature. That was part of the deal.

This wasn't that.

This was: You are mine to use. You stepped in my line. Now you're in my story and you don't get to step out.

"You need water," Mandy said, finally, because offering water felt like doing something. "Or tea. Do you want tea? I can make tea."

Mercedes didn't move. "Tea is for grandmas," she said weakly, not even adding the usual "no offense to grandmas."

"I'll get Coke then," Mandy said.

Mercedes didn't answer, which in Mercedes-language meant yes. Mandy stood, smoothed the bed cover uselessly around her friend's hip, and padded barefoot to the kitchen.

Her mother looked up from her chair at the table, where a stack of mail sat like a threat. She had her reading glasses halfway down her nose and that small crease between her eyebrows that appeared when she was doing numbers in her head and they weren't friendly.

"She's here again," her mother said quietly. It wasn't judgment. It was observation, plus: I am clocking this because it matters. "Is she staying?"

"She can," Mandy said. "If that's okay."

"It's okay," her mother said immediately. "Is she…?" She trailed off and made a face that tried to ask without asking. Hurt? Drunk? Scared? Pregnant? Harmed? Hungry? The set of possibilities for a sixteen-year-old girl in this city was a list no one ought to have memorized, and they had all memorized it anyway.

"She's just tired," Mandy lied. Then she amped the lie to something almost true. "Boy stuff."

Her mother's mouth softened in recognition. Boy stuff was believable. Boy stuff did not involve police or gangsters or potential crime activities.

"Got it," her mom said. She stood, opened the fridge, and started rummaging.

"Mom, I can—"

"I'm making you a plate," her mother said, in that tone that meant: I need to be helpful, please allow it. "Coke, yes. And some of that leftover chicken."

Mandy let her. She leaned on the counter and watched her mother work fast, efficient, like she was dressing a wound. It made something twist in Mandy's stomach in a way that had nothing to do with her own cramps.

"Do we like him?" her mother asked neutrally, arranging cold chicken and two slices of bread and a stack of cucumber like this was a café and not their kitchen.

"No," Mandy said, way too fast.

Her mother glanced at her. "Okay," she said. She didn't push. She assembled, poured, slid things onto a tray like room service in a nicer apartment than this.

When Mandy came back in with the tray, Mercedes had shifted onto her side, still curled, face now visible. Her eyes were red but dry. That was its own warning sign. When Mercedes cried for real, it was loud, a stormfront. This dry-red was something worse.

"Room service," Mandy announced softly, setting the tray down on the bedside table like they were mock-playing hotel and like nothing in the world could touch them here.

Mercedes let her arm fall away from her face, just enough to squint at the Coke. "Bless," she whispered, grabbing it and taking a long pull like it was medicine.

"Also chicken," Mandy said. "And cucumber. Which is basically water but crunchy."

Mercedes made a face and reached for the chicken with slow fingers. She ate without tasting like she just remembered she had a body that needed fuel and it would be rude to let it fail.

They sat in companionable fake-normal silence for two minutes. Mandy listened to the tiny sounds: swallow, fizz, the click of her own cheap clock on the desk. Her phone was on the floor, screen down, like an animal she did not trust and did not want to provoke.

Mercedes finally spoke. She didn't look at Mandy when she did it; she stared at a crack in the ceiling that looked like a river on a map. "He doesn't like me," she said.

"I know," Mandy said, because pretending otherwise would be insulting. Then she added, "Not like... like you wanted him to. Not like that."

Mercedes swallowed more Coke and nodded. "I thought... I thought he did. The way he looked. I thought I was... special?" She laughed a little at herself and it wasn't kind. "That's embarrassing."

"It's not," Mandy said. "He made you feel like that on purpose. That's how guys like him make people do things. That's not you being dumb. That's him being a manipulative... rat."

"Rat is weak," Mercedes said. "He's more like a... snake with WiFi."

Mandy made a small noise of agreement.

Mercedes let out a breath that almost became a laugh, but then it shook apart. "He's going to hurt her," she whispered.

Mandy didn't ask who *her* was. She didn't have to. Mercedes's mom wasn't a mom, not really. She was a door that sometimes opened and sometimes didn't. But she was still *hers*. You don't have to be good to be worth protecting.

"No," Mandy said. Like she could say it into reality. "We're going to do this, and he's not going to touch her, and then he's going to leave you alone."

Mercedes gave her a look that translated to *you don't believe that any more than I do*. But she nodded. Nodding was easier than screaming.

"He's just another man," Mercedes said into the blanket. "Another man who thinks... we're props."

Mandy went still. That landed. "He is," she said quietly.

They sat like that, the tray between them, the air buzzing faintly with that aftertaste of threat, for a long time. Eventually, Mercedes's eyes closed. She didn't sleep-sleep. She did the thing where your brain stands like a guard at the gate of sleep and says, *You can sit, but you can't lie down.* Mandy sat on the floor and kept watch anyway, even though watching didn't fix anything. It felt like the only thing she could do.

When Mercedes's breathing evened out, Mandy reached for her phone. She flipped it over slowly, already bracing.

No new messages from Bilal. None from the unknown number. Just memes from a class group chat and school announcements and a notification from Olle where he'd sent her a photo of some random science stuff she had no energy to pretend to be enthusiastic about.

Her stomach clenched. She put the phone face down again like a guilty secret.

Her brain started whispering the thing she didn't want to think yet: *We need help*. But from who? Adults? The cops? Teachers? She thought of telling Ms. von Post anything about what Bilal had said. The thought made her feel weirdly exposed, like an insect on a glass slide.

No. Not von Post. No matter how cool she was, she was just a science teacher, not some federal agent.

Someone who fights back, she thought. Someone who hates these guys already, and not in a "boys suck" way but in an *I have files on you* way.

Her mind flicked to the news clips: the ones with the serious forensic tech standing just out of the frame where they'd blurred the body, gloved hands, tight mouth, eyes that didn't smile for the camera. For a second, Mandy let herself imagine going up to someone like that and just... handing this problem over. Here. Take it. Handle it. Be the adult that none of the adults in my actual life can be.

Then she pictured police stations and statements and "We'll look into it" and Mercedes's mother's face meeting a wall, and the fantasy dropped out from under her.

No help, then. Just them. For now.

Mandy leaned her head back against the bed and closed her eyes. The sleep that came was thin and busy, full of red numbers flickering at the edges of her vision and her dad silently pointing, *look, look, look*. But she couldn't figure out: at what?

∧∨∧

Mandy woke to the feeling that someone had set a glass of cold water on her chest and it was slowly sinking through her ribs. The room was dark except for the rectangular bruise of streetlight on the floor. For a confused second she thought she'd left music on, there was a hum in the air, thin as a mosquito, but then she realized it was the blood in her ears.

Her phone lay beside her pillow, face-down. She didn't touch it. She didn't have to. Red light bled through the thin gap between case and screen like it was leaking. She reached, flipped it over with two fingers, and the numbers were already there, too big for the glass, as if they'd been projected from somewhere else and her phone was just catching them: **41:07:23 → 41:07:22 → 41:07:21**.

Her breath snagged.

"Dad?" she whispered before she even saw him, and then she did, there, in the shallow space between her desk and the wardrobe, where there wasn't room for a person to stand but he was standing anyway. Same jacket. He was not ghostly see-through, not movie fog; solid enough that her brain refused to accept it and accepted it at the same time.

His mouth didn't move. His eyes met hers and did that soft thing that always both broke and built her in the same second.

"Dad?" she said, too loud in the small room, the word leaving her like a cough. "Dad, are you—"

He didn't shush her. He didn't say anything. He lifted his hand, palm angled down like he was smoothing air, and then pointed, not at her, not at the door, but at the phone in her hand. The red ticks chopped another second off. **41:07:11.**

"What are you trying to tell me?" Her voice cracked into a whisper because yelling at a miracle felt like bad manners. "Are you real? Are you a ghost? Are you—" She made a frustrated noise that wasn't a word. "Please... say something. Please."

His mouth shaped a word she couldn't hear. It could have been *look*. It could have been *run*. It could have been *sorry*. He pointed again at the phone, slower, as if the meaning was all there and she was the one choosing not to see.

"Dad!" She leaned forward so fast the mattress groaned. "Don't go, don't—"

The overhead light stuttered once as if the bulb hiccupped, and in the blink between bright and dim he wasn't there anymore.

He was gone.

Her nose prickled, then flooded. Warmth over her lip. She jerked, half sitting, palm to face, and came away with scarlet. The room pulsed sideways for a second, a soft tilt like the floor had rolled under her.

"Okay," she whispered to the dark, to herself. "Okay. Okay." She pinched the bridge of her nose and swung her legs over the side of the bed. The phone screen had gone ordinary, dumb and blank, the way a cat looks away when you try to catch it misbehaving.

She made it to the door by feeling her way along furniture like the room had forgotten where she usually kept things. Her fingers found the knob. The hall felt colder, like the air had edges. She moved soft, careful not to wake her mom. The only light came from the kitchen: a wedge of yellow under the door, the murmur of a chair leg resisting when someone shifted their weight.

Water, she told herself, like it was a mission. Water, napkin, tissue, upright posture, act normal.

She pushed the door open and the kitchen unfolded, familiar and safe as a bedtime story. The table, with its old burn ring from when her mom put a pan down too hot and said *well, that's a comet, then*. The fridge hum like a sleeping animal. And Olle, at the table, in his hoodie, a bowl cupped in his hands like he was warming them on it. Cereal at midnight, of course. His hair stuck up at the back like a little crown of thorns, and his eyes were softer than they got at school. He looked up with exactly the level of surprise appropriate to seeing his sister appear with blood on her face at 2-something in the morning: minimal, but alert.

"Hey," he said, like they were in a library. He set the spoon down without clinking it. "You're bleeding."

"Thanks," she said, grabbing a paper towel and pressing it under her nose. The room swam a little less. "I noticed."

He watched her for three silent seconds that stretched into something like care. "Sit," he said finally. "If you stand your heart beats faster and you get more pressure. That's... obvious."

She sat. The chair made its usual chirp against the floor; the sound was absurdly comforting. She tilted her head a tiny bit forward like Google once told her and tried to breathe through her mouth.

Olle pushed the cereal toward her. "Do you want the milk?" he asked. "I can pour it back and get you water."

"Water," she said. "Please."

He stood, poured, set a glass by her elbow like a lab assistant setting down a solvent. Then he leaned his hip against the counter and regarded her with the frank curiosity of someone who observed before he judged. His eyes flicked to the paper towel, to the way her hand shook, to the faint smear of red she'd missed on her upper lip. He passed a napkin across the table without comment. She wiped. The humiliation of being messy in front of anyone faded in his quiet.

"I think I'm... seeing things," she said.

Olle didn't flinch. He didn't rush. He just waited, which was his superpower. The way some people made you feel like you were running out of time, Olle made time widen until your words could walk through it without tripping.

She kept her voice low because the apartment carried sound in weird ways at night. "I saw Dad. Again." Saying it felt like stepping onto thin ice and daring it to hold. "He—he doesn't talk. He just—he points. At my phone. It's—" She lifted her phone like she needed to prove the phone was real. The screen was normal now. Her lock screen, boring and harmless. "It shows this... countdown. Big numbers. Red. And he points at it. And then he's gone." Her throat closed for a second. She forced it open. "I think I'm hallucinating. Or—" Her eyes stung. She blinked hard. The tears went where tears go when you don't let them be seen. "I miss him."

Olle's gaze softened in a way that made her want to cry more, which she resented. He tilted his head a little, a bird listening for a tremor. "Since when?" he asked. Not *are you sure*. Not *that's crazy*. Just data collection.

"Three days?" she said. "No—longer. I don't know. It's like sleep is holes now. I wake up and it's there and then it's not." She swallowed. "Tonight it said forty-three hours."

"Forty-three hours to what?" Olle asked, not with sarcasm but with genuine curiosity, like he was at the start of a math problem that might be fun later.

"I don't know." The frustration came out sharp. "If I knew I wouldn't be in the kitchen at two a.m. bleeding on paper towels."

"Okay," he said. He reached for the cereal again and then didn't. He pushed the bowl further away, aligning it precisely with the table edge because the universe felt better when straight lines were straight. "Did anything else happen? Besides the bleeding?"

She thought. "I... the room went weird. Like... lag. And I felt lightheaded. And—" She shut her eyes, rewound, hit play. "Sometimes when it happens, I blink and then it's like... time slipped? Like I missed a few seconds? Like it happened once in the hallway and I looked up and the clock at school is just... later. And I don't know how I got from one second to the next."

Olle's eyes lit in that quiet way that meant the inside of his head had just turned on six lamps. "Skip-seconds," he murmured, tasting the phrase. "Phase lag."

"What?"

He was already pushing his chair back. He moved like a careful storm, deliberate, contained. At the counter he pulled open the junk drawer, the one that held pens that only worked if you scribbled on the corner of a receipt first, rubber bands that had gone brittle, a screwdriver, a pink birthday candle, three dead AA batteries, and two good ones. He found a pen, tested it, nodded to himself, then padded out and returned with his grid notebook, the one she always teased him about because it looked like a book of secrets from a conspiracy theorist except all the secrets were math.

He flipped to a fresh page and wrote in clean block letters:

MANDY — Δτ LEDGER

Below it, he drew columns:

DATE | TIME (A) | COUNTDOWN (B) | Δt = A vs B | SYMPTOMS | CONTEXT

He turned the notebook so it faced her. "We should write them down," he said. "All of them. When. What it said. What you felt. Where you were. If anything else was happening. If the lights flickered. If there was a blast that day." He tapped gently at **Δt**. "You said it said forty-three hours tonight. When did it start? Did it jump? Because I think maybe... the numbers aren't just numbers. They must mean something... " He stopped.

Mandy stared at the columns like they were a joke in a foreign language. "You don't think I'm crazy," she said, and it came out more like a question than she meant.

Olle blinked. "I think you're Mandy." He said it like a fact he could measure.

The paper towel in her hand had gone soft. "Maybe we are both crazy," She whispered, folding it into a smaller square just to have something to do. "What if it's just grief making pictures?" she asked, voice small. "People see dead people sometimes. Like... in movies. Or when they're broken."

Olle didn't argue. He considered. "It could be," he said. "But if it is... then writing it down, will make it worse?" He tilted his head, then shook it. "No. If it is grief, then the numbers won't make sense. If it isn't... then they might."

She let out a breath she didn't know she was holding. The hope she'd been bullying into silence all week lifted its head, wary.

He held the pen out. "Tell me what it said tonight. Exact."

She told him. He wrote all of it down, the time she woke up, the numbers. The gesture Dad made.

She thought of the way her room had felt like it had dimmed from the inside. "The room did not flicker," she said. "More like... the air turned to dark for a second. That sounds stupid."

He shook his head. "Not stupid." He drew a tiny star. "Air dark."

He kept writing like that calmed him, because it did, and she watched his neat letters and felt something in her ribcage unknot half a turn. It didn't fix anything. It didn't make her dad stay when he came. But it made the edges of the fear less jagged.

"Will you..." She cleared her throat. "Will you not tell Mom?"

He met her eyes, steady. "I won't tell anyone," he said. It wasn't conspiratorial. It was a promise in the shape of a period.

"Thanks," she said, and the word had weight.

He tapped the top of the page again. "Next time it happens," he said, "if you can—if you're not too... dizzy—take a picture. Or write the number down right then. Or just say it out loud and record a voice note. And if you feel... more lag, or if you skip-seconds, sit down. Don't stand. Don't try stairs. And—" He hesitated, then added very gently, "If you start to lose more time than a few seconds... You tell me."

She nodded. The kitchen had that too-quiet feeling again, like it was listening. Somewhere outside, a drunk laughed, the sound floating up thin as paper. The city kept moving. Of course it did.

"Okay," she said, and then again, because the word felt like a talisman, "okay."

Olle closed the notebook but kept his hand on it like a guard dog at rest. "You can sit with me," he said, a little awkward. "If you don't want to go back yet."

She looked at the dent in the table; then at his face, all angles and sincerity; then at the hallway, at the slice of her door visible beyond it. The thought of lying in the dark waiting for red numbers felt like a dare she didn't want to take.

"I'll sit," she said.

He nodded, satisfied, and slid the cereal bowl back to center. He pushed it toward her like an offering. "Want some? It's gross," he added, which was true—soggy—"but it's food."

She surprised herself by taking a spoonful. It was, in fact, gross. She ate it anyway. They sat together like that, and after a while, her heart found a normal rhythm. The bleeding stopped completely. The cold water in her glass warmed to room temperature and she didn't mind. Olle began drawing a tiny triangle in the margin of the notebook, then another, as if his hand couldn't help itself. She didn't ask why.

When she finally stood to go back to bed, Olle tore a narrow strip from the corner of the page and slid it to her. On it, in his tidy print, he'd written:

Rules for When It Happens

1. Sit down. Breathe.

2. Note the time. Say the number out loud if you can.

3. If you can, photo/voice note once.

4. Tell Olle.

She read it twice. It looked so ordinary, like a list for groceries. It made the not-ordinary feel slightly tamer.

"Okay," she said, folding the strip and tucking it into her phone case. "Goodnight."

"Night," he said. He started to say something else but then he just nodded. Maybe what he'd been about to say was *I miss him too.*

In her room, Mandy closed the door softly. The bed was still warm on one side where fear had been sleeping. She lay down, phone facedown on the rug again like a truce. She waited for red. None came.

For the first time all week, when she closed her eyes, the numbers didn't crowd the inside of her lids. She dreamed of nothing, which felt like the kindest thing.

Down the hall, Olle stared at the triangle he'd sketched and didn't know why he'd drawn it, only that it felt... necessary. He wrote a single word under it: **Window**. Then he clicked his pen closed like the end of a prayer and turned the page.

CHAPTER 7

Aldina had never liked the overhead lights in the station. Too cold. Too interrogational. They made everyone look guilty. Now, at 23:40, they hummed over her head in the briefing room while her chief droned on, reading out "areas of improvement" like a grocery list.

"...and frankly," he was saying, tapping on a printout he didn't understand, "we're not delivering. We're not getting the prosecutions. We are seeing repeat offenders back out. The public perception right now is that we cannot control this wave of explosions, and we—"

It tuned into static in her ears. She'd heard this song before, too many verses. It always sounded the same: the bosses above her were getting yelled at by the bosses above them, who were getting yelled at by politicians on TV who were getting yelled at by a public that had seen one too many front doors blown in at 02:00. The anger rolled downhill. It always seemed to stop right on top of her.

She could tell when the speech ended because everyone in the room sat up and did the polite shuffle, collecting binders, nodding with faces set to *serious professional concern*. Aldina did it too, because it was easier than not.

"Stay back a second," her chief said, like a teacher keeping someone after class.

Of course.

When the others cleared out, he leaned on the table and pinched the bridge of his nose, like his face hurt and it was partly her fault and partly the fault of gravity. "This last one," he said. "The hallway blast. The judge wrote 'transferable DNA.' Do you know how bad that looks? We bring you in on gunshot work, on post-scene analysis, we fight for funding for your lab, and then when it hits court the guy walks because 'transferable DNA.'"

She could recite the answer in her sleep. "He walked," she said evenly, "because the prosecutor failed to contextualize the DNA pattern. The spatter direction on the wall told a story. They didn't tell it."

"The spatter," he echoed, like it was a hobby, like she'd said "my knitting."

"Yes," she said. "The spatter."

He rubbed his face harder. "Listen. I'm on your side, okay? But we can't keep bringing people in and losing them because you're too technical to explain things to a jury."

Her jaw flexed. "With respect, sir, I am not the one explaining things to a jury. I am the one collecting what's left after other people ruin a hallway."

He didn't like that. She watched it cross his face and land. "Just... fix it," he said finally. "We can't afford another miss."

He left her in the hum.

She stared at the empty doorway for a long beat. Then, quietly, to the quiet room, she said, "I'm twenty-five. I'm not God."

She said it with no drama because she didn't believe in drama. Drama got you sloppy; sloppy got evidence thrown out. She believed in method. She believed in cold.

Her résumé read like someone older. Säpo internship when she was nineteen, "potential fast-tracker." Transfer to Major Crimes at twenty-one. Field work on gun deaths, arson, micro-blasts. She'd been patted on the head a lot by men who thought they were praising her when they said things like "impressive at your age." She didn't care about their patting. She cared about the files that closed with no conviction and another mother who had to identify a body.

Her father's file was one of those.

They called it an accident. Faulty boiler. City bus depot maintenance failure. That's how it appeared in the system: *Unintentional fatality due to mechanical malfunction.* No suspect. No charges. Open-and-shut.

Except the scorch pattern had been wrong. The residue had told a different story. She'd seen the photos later, after she'd gotten to the right level of clearance—and after she'd cried all her tears in one night and sworn not to again. She'd marked it out herself: angle of force, residue spread, secondary ignition. It hadn't been a boiler that killed him. It had been a test charge. A baby bomb. One of a string.

And no one cared. Not then. "Resources," they'd said. "Priorities."

So she cared. And she never stopped.

∧∨∧

In her apartment, she didn't bother with the overhead light. She flicked on the desk lamp. A clean circle of white lit her wall, and the wall lit her, and that was enough.

The wall looked like madness and felt like order. Photos taped up in messy grids. Names, some full, some just street names. Places. Cross streets. Printouts of Google Maps with markers she'd penciled in hard enough to dent the paper. Scene photos: scorch marks, blast radii. She'd printed them in black and white, partly to save color ink, mostly because grayscale made them feel less like raw meat. Red thread laced from photo to photo. It wasn't for show. It helped her see pathways, pressure points. She didn't care if it looked like a conspiracy board in a bad TV crime show. She hadn't built it for TV.

The faces on the wall were mostly young men. Some alive. Some dead. Some with their eyes open and daring the camera to do something; some with their eyes closed forever, heads tilted at angles no one's head should ever tilt. The city had too many of those angles now. Judges were starting to call those murders "volume crime" under their breath, like vandalism. As if that made it less obscene.

At the center of the web, where the threads got thickest and most knotted, was a printout of a blurry screengrab from earlier that spring: a kid in a black puffer, hood up, jaw set, gaze soft in a way that didn't match the hardness of his mouth. Bilal Hernandez.

Underneath, in block letters, she'd printed: **BILAL — ACQUITTED** and, under that, in smaller hand, like a footnote to herself: *judge called DNA transferable.*

Bull-fucking-shit.

Aldina sat in the only chair in her place that felt like it belonged to her: straight-backed, hard, built for work, not lounging. Her sofa existed for people who wanted to pretend they were visiting a normal person. No one did, so the sofa stayed showroom neat.

She looked at Bilal's face on the wall and let her anger unclench slowly, like releasing a fist one finger at a time so you didn't sprain anything.

"I know you," she said quietly to the photo. "And I know what you've done. And even if the judge likes saying 'transferable DNA' like it means 'magic exoneration', you still did it. You still pulled that trigger many times. You were in that stairwell when the old man caught a stray. You stood look-out on the daycare blast. Don't act like you didn't."

Her jaw tensed. She thought of the mothers. The children. Herself included.

"But you're not the one designing this," she added, even softer. "Are you."

That was new. That was the voice that had started talking in her head over the last few weeks. The pattern on the wall had changed. Or... grown more prominent. The blasts were increasing in frequency but also shifting in placement, triangles, as if someone were connecting specific points on a quiet map. That wasn't turf war. That wasn't "he said he disrespected me so we lit his corner." That was... strategic.

Which meant someone above Bilal. Which meant Bilal wasn't the end of the line. Which meant her aim: cornering him alone in a stairwell and making sure he never hurt anyone again wasn't enough. Now she needed more information.

It was almost funny, in a sick way. She had wanted so badly to blame one face. She had wanted a single villain. That was clean. That was doable. You could wrap your hands around one neck in your imagination. You could whisper Code 6004 and call it justice.

Code 6004. Her private mantra. Death without suspicion of crime.

That's what they wrote when someone just... died. Fell. Stopped breathing. Slipped in the bath. Not a homicide, no investigation. Box ticked, case closed.

She'd been rolling it around in her head more lately than was healthy. She knew that. *If someone dangerous died quietly, if someone who was going to kill again just went to sleep and didn't wake up... and if the report called it 6004... would that really be wrong? Or would that be mercy?*

She stared at Bilal's face and whispered it now, under her breath, like a test. "Six-zero-zero-four."

The number tasted metallic in her mouth.

"Would you deserve that?" she asked the wall. She leaned back in the chair until the top edge dug into her shoulder blades. She ran two fingers over the old burn scar she carried HIGH on her forearm, the one her father used to kiss and say, *You're my little soldier.* She was sixteen when he said that. He died two months later in what they said was a "boiler accident."

"Dad," she said softly, not looking at his photo, "you'd tell me not to. You'd say the law matters. You always said that."

Her throat tightened. "But what if the law is asleep?"

The wall did not answer, obviously. But her mind did what it always did. It started clearing, sharpening, weaponizing grief into grid lines.

If she couldn't trust the system to stop Bilal, she'd do it herself.

That had been the plan. That was *still* the plan. But the plan had gotten muddy now. Because here was the thing: the logical part of her brain knew that Bilal wasn't a free agent. Despite all he had been a part of, you couldn't chalk all the crime as a part of delinquents' hobby. The way the explosions were landing told her that. Somebody was placing them with intent. Somebody who knew infrastructure maps. Somebody who knew how to hit a stairwell so you got press coverage, and then how to hit a business so you got fear, and then how to hit a mostly empty delivery hub at 3:00 a.m. so you got practice.

Practice. That was what made her stomach turn.

Practice for something bigger.

She rubbed her eyes with the heel of her hand and sat forward again. Paper rustled under her palm. On her desk lay a small stack of incident printouts, fresh from that evening. Industrial road. Two teenage girls spotted running from a mall shoplifting attempt less than an hour before, only to be cornered by Bilal.

Girls.

Her pen hovered over that line, like a dowsing rod. She underlined *two teenage girls* and wrote in the margin: **RECRUITMENT? COURIERS?** Her stomach clenched. "Ghost couriers." That was the slang the gang unit used, half-joking, to talk about girls who carried packages because nobody clocked girls as threats. She'd heard the term so often it had stopped feeling like a horror. Now it punched her in the throat.

Her mind contextualized without asking permission: young, scared-looking, running. Not hardened. Not part of a known crew. Pulled in because they were convenient. But convenient for whom? Who was playing the strings behind Bilal?

Something inside her, already tight with anger, cinched two notches tighter. She shook her head. It didn't matter. Regardless of the bigger picture, Bilal had too much blood and soot on his hands.

The decision bloomed inside her like heat. It wasn't a snap. It was something that had been growing in her, patient and slow, suddenly showing leaves. She was not going to wait for paperwork. She was not going to hope a reluctant prosecutor cared enough to translate the science. She was not going to sit politely through another dressing-down from her chief about "transferable DNA."

She picked up a thumbtack with her free hand and pressed a new printout to the corner of the board: a city map with three points circled. She stretched a red thread between them. It formed a clean triangle. Her pulse ticked up. She marked the center with a pen.

Her lips moved around a whisper. "What are you doing," she asked the invisible someone above all this. "And why are you practicing?"

The wall, as usual, stayed silent.

But she knew this much: whatever they were practicing for, it wasn't just random street beef. It wasn't just some kid playing gangster for Instagram clout. It was patient, directional, building.

And if Bilal was in that chain even one link, then she needed to know what he knew... before she made sure he wouldn't harm a single hair on anyone's head ever again.

Still, she tasted the number on her tongue again like a test of who she was becoming.

"Six-zero-zero-four," she breathed.

It did not feel like justice yet. It felt like a line she hadn't crossed. Yet.

She was going to find Bilal. She was going to lock him down. She was going to stop him, whatever that had to mean, because if she didn't, some sixteen-year-old girl was going to be standing near a blast she'd been forced to carry to its drop point. And then what? Another mother holding pieces. Another useless press conference.

"This is justice," she told herself, because you had to call it something. "This is prevention."

Even as she said it, she felt the line she was about to cross, like a curb in the dark.

Her eyes went back to Bilal's photo. His expression in it, frozen from a grainy still, wasn't cocky. That was the irritating part. He didn't look smug. He looked... tired. Focused. And, if she let herself really look: scared. She didn't like that. It made the math worse.

But this was about the math of a broken system.

If the system wouldn't protect its people, then she would.

And if that meant getting there before the cops, before the prosecutor, before the paperwork... Well, Code 6004 was just a number.

CHAPTER 8

The text came just after dusk, when the city turned into a flicker book of windows and headlights and people moving fast because moving slowly felt like asking to be seen. Mandy was helping her mom stack plates from the dishwasher when her phone buzzed and crawled across the counter like it wanted to jump.

Unknown:
Tomorrow. Late. Silos.

Another buzz, before she could even decide whether to breathe.

Unknown:
Bring her.

No noise. No one else. Don't reply.

Mandy didn't need the contact saved. The rhythm of the words was already in her bones. She wiped her hand on a dish towel she wasn't using and slid the phone under her sleeve like it had a temperature.

"Everything okay?" her mother asked, not looking up from the plate she was drying.

"Yeah," Mandy said. Too fast. Then slower: "Just Mercedes."

Her mother's mouth curved, that soft sympathetic smile she had for Mercedes—like Mercedes was more stray cat than girl. "She can stay over if she needs," she said, the way other people said, *We have milk.*

Mandy nodded, and the nod was gratitude, and also a plea she didn't say out loud: *Keep allowing this. Keep saying yes even if you don't know exactly what you're saying yes to.*

In the hallway, she texted. Not Bilal. Mercedes.

Mandy:
He wrote.

Three dots for a long time, which meant Mercedes was throwing her phone on the bed and storming around the room and then grabbing the phone again and then dropping it again.

Mercedes:
What's he want?

Mandy:
Silos. Tomorrow. Late.

A pause. Then:

Mercedes:
Okay. We go.

Mandy:
I know.

The "I know" seemed to take some of the voltage out of Mercedes's typing. A sticker came back, a cat in sunglasses. Then a second buzz.

Mercedes:
I can't tell if I want to punch him or hug him. That's so dumb.

Mandy:
It's not dumb.
It's the spell. He knows how to do spells.

Mercedes:
Then we break his wand.

Mandy smiled, grim and brief. She slid the phone into her hoodie pocket and went back to the kitchen to say she was going to shower. She wasn't. She needed to sit with the way the words *Silos. Tomorrow. Late* had opened up a hole under her. She needed to plan what it meant to walk out onto a plank and not look down.

∧∨∧

The silos were a place your mom told you never to go and the internet told you never to geotag. The road out there wasn't exactly *industrial,* it was more like someone had broken off pieces of industry and left them lying around. Concrete towers with their own weather. Chain-link fences with signs that had been sun-bleached into resignation. A strip of scrub grass that fought the idea of concrete like it took it personally.

They went by moped, because that felt less... official. Mandy clamped her hands on Mercedes's waist and tried not to watch the city peel away, layer by layer: the baker with the taped crack in the window, the tram stop that still smelled like smoke, the café with the chalkboard that said *Card Only* like cash had started a fight there.

Night out by the silos didn't look like night in the city. It felt older. The air didn't have the scent of fried everything. It smelled like iron and damp and the memory of grain, even though nothing living went in those towers now except gulls. The wind off the water pulled at Mandy's hoodie strings and tried to tug a shiver up her spine.

He was already there.

Bilal leaned against the shadowed base of one of the towers like he lived there, like the concrete had grown him. Night made his angles sharper and his age murkier. He wasn't a man in his thirties and he wasn't a boy, and sometimes the space between those facts looked like a knife.

"Hi," Mercedes said, too bright, like that would fling light onto him and make him safer. The brightness wobbled and righted itself. "You picked the most romantic spot."

"No one listens here," he said. His voice didn't echo. It slid into the concrete and stayed there. He flicked his eyes over Mandy— counting, as always, *just the two of you*—then back to Mercedes. The flicker of something troubled his mouth, then smoothed out. "Phone."

They both handed them over without arguing. He toggled them to airplane mode, then set them screen down on the hood of a dead-white delivery van with a flat tire, like he was tucking small animals down for a nap.

"It's... late," Mandy said, because saying something helped.

"And you came," he said, like they'd passed a test he wasn't sure he wanted them to pass.

"Was that in doubt?" Mercedes asked, somewhere between taunt and invitation. The wind teased strands of her hair into her lip gloss and she swiped them back with a small annoyed gesture that made his eyes flicker again.

Bilal's chin tipped toward the far side of the yard, where a fence had been peeled up and not put back down properly. "In there." he said, nodding toward the gap like it could speak. "In the paint shed. Behind the loose panels. There will be a satchel. You need to pick it up tomorrow at eight in the evening." He looked at Mandy, then Mercedes, making sure the words hit bone. "You go in, you pick it up, you walk. No running, no looking around. No heroes. You take it to an abandoned alley in the city center to stash it closer to you— you will get the location, and then you'll get a text when and where to drop it after a few days. That's it."

"That's not it," Mercedes said, like she couldn't help it. "Why us?"

He smiled then, and it hurt to look at because it didn't reach anywhere near his eyes. "Because no one sees you," he said. "Until they do. You look like you're shopping. You look like you're late for a movie. You look like you're too busy looking at yourselves in your phones to be doing anything that matters."

"We matter," Mercedes said, fiercely.

He blinked. "I didn't say you didn't."

Silence tried to creep in. Mandy watched it, the way you watch a cat that might decide to scratch you for petting it wrong. "How heavy is it?" she asked. A practical question was a way to keep control of air.

"Heavy," he said. "On purpose."

"On purpose?" Mandy asked.

"So you feel it," he said, and something bleak flickered over his face so fast she almost missed it. "So you don't forget."

"Forget what?" Mercedes asked, chin up.

He held her eyes for two beats. "That you're carrying something that cannot be messed with," he said. He didn't say the word *bomb* and he didn't have to. The wind carried it anyway and scraped it along the concrete.

Mercedes's laugh came out thin. "That's not... romantic."

"Romance is for containers with nothing in them," he said. And then, softer, like he wished the softness would turn on him and bite him for showing up: "Don't open it. No matter what. Don't mess with it. Don't try to be smart. You open it, it learns you. You open it, it wants to sing."

Mandy's stomach tightened as if she'd understood the language of that warning exactly. "We're not trying to be smart," she said.

"You are," he said. "It's who you are. Try to be *obedient* instead."

Mercedes's mouth made a shape like shut up, you don't get to say that. She didn't let the words out. She asked a different question. "And if we don't?" she said. "If we don't pick it up?"

He looked past them into the dark like the answer was there. When he looked back, whatever had flickered in his face earlier was gone. His jaw was steadier. "You know better than to ask that question," he said mildly to Mercedes.

Mandy glanced at Mercedes and swallowed. "Of course, we don't need it spelled out."

"Good," he said. "Because I don't like saying it."

"You don't like a lot of things you do," Mercedes said, and there was the push again, the dangerous almost-flirt where rage and wanting wore the same lipstick.

Something in him flinched, almost invisible. Then it hardened, and the hardness wasn't theatrical. It was infrastructure. "Be at the fence when I tell you," he said. "No earlier. You go in. You take it. You walk."

"And the drop text?" Mandy asked. "Who sends it?"

His mouth tugged. "The air," he said, the words were sarcastic but his tone wasn't. Then, less poetic: "You'll get it."

He stepped in closer then—not menacing, just... nearer. Close enough for Mercedes to see the small scar along his jaw she hadn't noticed before, like someone had cut him there and the wound had become part of his face the way a story becomes part of the version you tell of yourself.

"You ever peeled a sticker off a new phone?" he asked, out of nowhere.

Mercedes blinked at him. "What?"

"The sticker," he said. "The protective one. The clean peel. It's satisfying. It makes you want to do it again. Don't be that person," he said. "Don't peel anything. Don't... investigate. Don't 'what if' it. Don't make it yours."

"You keep telling us not to be who we are," Mercedes said, quietly.

He looked like he was going to answer, and Mandy didn't want to know what it would be. She took a half step back. "We should go," she said. "Tomorrow is school."

He reached past them and picked up their phones from the van hood. He canceled airplane mode and set them gently in their open hands like he was returning glass birds he'd borrowed.

"You see anything weird on your way in," he said, "you leave. You don't play detective."

"I like detectives," Mercedes said. "In shows."

"Shows end," he said. "That's the difference."

He didn't watch them leave. That was the strangest thing. He turned and looked up at the silo, like the concrete had finally started talking to him and he wanted to hear.

They walked. The night had teeth. Mandy didn't realize she was holding her phone so tightly until her fingers started to ache. When they reached the moped, she let out a breath so slow it was almost nothing.

"Are we..." Mercedes started. "Are we really going to..."

"I don't know," Mandy said, because there was no soft-edged version of the truth.

ΛVΛ

They didn't sleep. Not really. Not the kind that cleans you. Mandy lay on her side and watched her window frame flatten into a rectangle of gray as morning arrived like a polite knock.

The day did its normal tricks. School. Bells. The long eyelash of a hair caught in her locker hinge. Mercedes snorting at a teacher's new haircut under her breath and then writing, *stop me* in Mandy's notebook margin with a heart. Mandy pretended to be held together by glue and a schedule.

Under the schedule, the day had a second clock, the one that made your skin too tight. Every hour closer to eight felt like walking deeper into a house you knew had a hole in the floor.

Unknown:
[Location]. There's a loose block in the alley. Behind the dumpster. Stash it there.

They didn't go home first. Home felt like leaving fingerprints on a plan. They roamed around the city to pass time, and then took the long way, letting the city thin out around them— streetlights farther apart, bikes chained to things nobody would steal, a lone cat with somebody else's ear. They parked the moped behind a rust-sprayed metal container and walked the last fifty meters because engines announce and feet don't.

"Phone," Mandy said, and held hers up. "We keep them on. Low brightness. If something happens, I need my camera fast."

"You and that camera," Mercedes said, half-annoyed, half-reverent. Mandy's phone camera had become a kind of talisman: *proof that nobody would believe if they didn't love you.*

They came to the fence. It still sulked, propped half up, like whoever had lifted it had been too lazy or too urgent to finish the job. The wind plucked at the loose chain-link and made it sing a high tinny note.

"You ready?" Mandy asked.

"Ask me after," Mercedes said.

They ducked under, breath holding itself like a game, and straightened up into a hush that didn't belong to them. The paint shed crouched twenty meters away: concrete cinderblock, flaking door. Someone had tagged a cartoon devil on the side with a roller instead of a spray can, thick and sloppy, as if even the graffiti artist had been in a hurry to be someplace else.

Inside, their eyes took a beat to turn on. The space smelled like old solvent and damp cardboard. Stacks of panels leaned against one inside wall like awkward guests lined up at a party. The floor was littered with screws and a spilled constellation of dried paint chips in colors no one would ever pick on purpose.

"Loose panels," Mercedes whispered, remembering. "Behind the loose panels."

Mandy ran her fingers along the edges, listening with her skin. One stack wobbled under her touch. She slid two panels aside with care, slow and steady so nothing scraped, and there it was: a satchel, plain, gray, like the kind of bag a man with a boring job might carry to work, except the language of its seams said *specialized.*

"It looks like a dad bag," Mercedes hissed. "Like receipts are in there."

Mandy didn't touch it. Not yet. She crouched and leaned close and listened. That felt ridiculous and also not. She heard nothing. No clockwork click. No hiss. No whisper. Just the small echo of her own breath coming back at her from concrete.

"Okay," she said. "We're going to—"

The air shivered.

It wasn't a sound. It was an idea that sound had decided not to show up and had sent its cousin instead. The light did a thing it didn't have the right to do: it slowed, then stuttered. The shed's corners seemed to inhale. The dust motes hung in place like they had forgotten how to fall.

And then he was there.

Her father.

He stood between the panels and the bag like he had walked into the wrong room looking for her and felt embarrassed about it. The ache that opened in Mandy started in her throat and dove. He wore the same clothes he always wore when he flickered into her. His face wasn't dreamy or ghost-blur. It was dangerously clear. It made tears start in her head and not make it to her eyes.

He didn't speak. He never spoke. He lifted his hand and pointed, not at the satchel, like she'd braced for, but at her phone.

Her phone woke up in her palm, she hadn't told it to. The lock screen dissolved into her map app, and the map wasn't showing where *they* were. It was showing three glowing pins, linked by a line that pulsed. A triangle she knew with a certainty that didn't belong to this room. One at the stairwell, the little café, the deserted doorway where glass still glittered in the cracks of the sidewalk. She could feel the exact places in her body. The line hummed toward a center that wasn't yet a point, like it was drawing itself as she watched.

Her father's finger traced it, slow and precise, like he was drawing it into her bones. The triangle held. Her breath did something bad. She could feel the tick in her head, that red countdown feel, hitch, then leap.

Her ears rang as if a fire alarm had started in another universe and she was getting the echo. Her stomach dipped like a stair had gone missing. She blinked.

When her eyes slid open, her father was gone, and the air remembered how to move.

"Mandy?" Mercedes said, voice high, alarmed. "You just— You were just—"

Mandy's back touched the wall. She didn't remember putting it there. "How long?" she asked. Her voice didn't sound like it belonged to her.

Mercedes fumbled her phone. "I don't... fifty seconds? More?"

Mandy swallowed against the dark metallic taste in her mouth and the pounding in her head. Her ears filled and emptied like someone was pressure-testing them with air. Mandy touched her upper lip and came away red. "Okay," she said, and it wasn't. "Okay. It's okay."

She lifted the phone with hands that made a lie of the word *steady* and tried to memorized the shape on the map that had disappeared with him, but the exact points had already decided to become ghosts. "Fuck," she whispered.

"What did you see?" Mercedes demanded, close enough now that Mandy could smell her gum and her fear.

"Triangle," Mandy said. "Three blasts. There's a center."

"Center what?"

"I don't know," Mandy said. "But it felt like... like 'go here.' Or 'don't let them go here.' I can't tell which. I'll show Olle."

Mercedes's face twisted. "Olle. Of course. We get a ghost geometry lesson and you want a tutor."

"He's not a tutor," Mandy said. "He's... he sees patterns. He can tell me if I'm imagining this."

"You're not imagining it," Mercedes said fiercely. "You went pale. And unresponsive. It felt like you were *gone,* like in a limbo."

"Just for a second," Mandy said.

"More like a minute," Mercedes said. "It freaked me out."

"Me too," Mandy said, and the honesty took her by surprise. "But we don't get to be freaked out right now. We have to finish the part where we don't die. Ready?"

Mercedes nodded, jaw set. "Ready."

Mandy slid her fingers under the satchel handle. It was colder than it had any right to be. When she lifted, the weight went up her arm into her shoulder and then sat there like a person had sat on her, or like guilt. Heavy, because *you're supposed to feel it.* She had the ruined thought that Bilal had set that line in her head on purpose. She pulled the strap up and slung it across her body so it pressed into her like a bruise waiting to be born.

"Walk," she said. "No running. No looking."

"I hate him," Mercedes whispered as they threaded the panels back into place. She didn't say who *him* was. There were too many candidates.

Outside, the night had that feeling it gets when something has decided it will happen and now the air is just waiting for you to catch up. They moved a little too fast and then remembered and moved the right amount. The satchel's weight pulled Mandy's steps into a new shape. She centered it with her hand like you would center a baby in a carrier you didn't trust yet.

A gull screamed and she almost dropped everything.

"Normal," she told her legs. "Be normal."

They ducked under the fence and straightened up into the damp and the road. No one shouted. No gates rolled. No sirens. The satchel made no sound but its own. They drove silently on the moped until they reached the dark alley hidden in the city center. There was only one dumpster, and yet the whole alley reeked of unpicked garbage.

They put it back. Like they had been asked. That was the worst part: seeing, touching, then leaving it somewhere else. Not tonight. Not now. They couldn't be over this that soon. But at the same time, it was also relieving. This was just a reconnaissance, not the actual sin. She and Mercedes slid the loose blocks behind the dumpster, slid their bodies out, slid their breath back into their throats. They left the alley and felt a small wrongness peel itself off their backs and hunker down behind them to watch them go.

Mandy's phone buzzed.

Unknown:
Good. You were quick.

She didn't type back. She didn't need to. Her palm typed *we're not yours to puppet around* into her bones, which wasn't the same as sending it.

They got on the moped. Mercedes turned the key. The engine choked and then agreed to live. They drove, and night fell off them in pieces, and the city took them back in like a giant mouth that didn't care if it bit.

CHAPTER 9

Mandy stared at her bedroom ceiling like it might start printing answers.

The house had gone soft and quiet in that way it did after ten: dishwasher hummed, TV murmured low from her mother's room, a tram sighed past outside like a tired animal. She should've been in bed pretending this day hadn't happened. Instead she was pacing grooves into the rug, replaying the shed, the satchel, her father's face too clear, the triangle burning inside her head like an afterimage from staring at the sun.

Fifty seconds gone.

Nose bleeding.

Metal in her mouth.

And that message: *Good. You were quick.*

She pressed her thumb hard into her phone's power button until the screen blinked off. It felt small and pathetic — like putting a band-aid on a bomb. Still, darkness helped.

She cracked her door and listened.

Her mother's door was closed. Light at the bottom: still awake. Mandy could hear the scrape of a chair; her mom moving around the kitchen for her nightly tea. It made Mandy hesitate.

If she walked out there now and said, *We got blackmailed by a gangster and moved a bag that is probably a bomb*, everything would explode. Police. Social services. Retaliation. Mercedes's drunk mother who wouldn't survive that kind of attention. Her own mom, fragile in ways she pretended not to see.

No.

The person she needed didn't slam or panic. He graphed.

She padded down the hall and stopped outside Olle's room.

No need to knock. If he was deep in something, he didn't hear anyway; if he wasn't, the sound would just knock the thought out of his head and she'd feel guilty.

She pushed the door open with two knuckles.

Olle sat at his desk, shoulders curled over a spread of paper. His lamp threw a narrow circle of cold light that made everything outside it look underwater. He was in his grey hoodie with the cuffs chewed ragged, a pencil balanced horizontally between his teeth. His notebook was open to a grid page dense with numbers and little notations in his cramped, identical handwriting.

On the far wall: printed maps. City layouts. Power lines. Bus routes. None of it looked random.

"You're going to run out of grids," she said softly.

He plucked the pencil from his mouth. "You can't run out of grids," he said, as if she'd suggested running out of triangles.

"Hi," she said.

"Hi," he echoed, eyes flicking to her face. He really looked then. His gaze always did this deliberate sweep: pupils, skin tone, shoulders, hands. Checking for damage. "Headache?" he asked.

"Yes," she admitted.

"Nosebleed?" he added.

She wiped under her nose on reflex. Clean now. "Earlier."

"How long were you gone?" he asked.

There it was. Not *What do you mean, gone?* He already had that category.

She closed the door behind her. The click sounded louder than it was.

"I don't know," she said. "Mercedes says almost a minute."

His mouth tightened. He reached for a new page, wrote $\Delta\tau$ at the top, then: $\approx$ **00:50**.

"You named it?" Mandy asked. "Of course you named it."

"Change in tau," he said. "Tau is proper time. Your time. Not the clock on the wall's time."

"You're such a freak," she said automatically.

"Yes," he agreed, already sketching. "Sit."

She did, dropping onto his bed. It squeaked in protest under the sudden weight of adrenaline plus satchel memory.

He turned halfway in his chair, the notebook still angled toward him. "Tell me everything," he said. "From the last time you told me to now. No edits."

He didn't say *No lying.* He didn't have to.

She chewed the inside of her cheek. "You remember the... the countdown," she started. "The red numbers on my phone. Seventy-two hours, then jumping down. And Dad. The... overlay." Even saying it out loud sounded stupid. Like she was describing a cheap filter.

He nodded. "You saw him again."

"In the shed by the silos," she said. "Where they left the—"

She cut herself off so hard the sentence snapped. He tilted his head.

"Mandy."

She shook her head. "I can't tell you all of it. Not because I don't trust you, okay? Because if you know and anything happens and they look through our phones or cameras or whatever, it's not just me and Mercedes anymore. It's you. And Mom. And her mom. People get... erased here for less."

He watched her, the muscle in his jaw ticking just once. "You already decided to tell me," he said. "You're here. So you have to choose: either I'm in or I'm out. Partial data is bad data."

"Stop sounding like Wikipedia," she snapped, more scared than annoyed.

He waited.

She exhaled, long, and twisted her fingers together. "Fine. In. But you swear on..." She glanced at his desk, hunting for something holy enough. "On your new graphing pens."

His eyes widened a little. Those pens were his dragon hoard. "Serious," he said.

"I'm serious," she said. "If you tell anyone, if you write it somewhere they can find, it's not just trouble. It's—" She swallowed. "They said things."

"Who," he asked, very calm.

"Bilal," she whispered.

Something changed in his face. A flicker like a page turning. "The guy from the station footage," he said quietly.

She blinked. "What?"

"Nothing," he said. "Continue."

She narrowed her eyes. Flagged that for later. "He's using us," she said. "Me and Mercedes. We didn't choose it. He picked us because we're invisible and we've been... stupid. Vapes, lip gloss, being where we shouldn't. He thinks that makes us his."

Olle's hands closed around his pencil. "What is he making you do?"

"Carry," she said. The word scraped. "We moved something for him tonight. We didn't open it. We're not allowed to open it. That's ... the point."

His nostrils flared once. "Is it drugs or explosives?"

"I'm not saying that word in this room," Mandy hissed. "In case your laptop is listening or whatever."

"Okay." He adjusted, like recalculating for wind. "You don't have to label the box. You're moving dangerous mass from Source to Target against your will."

"Yeah," she said. "That."

He took that in, no lecture, no you're-an-idiot. Just a small, sharp breath through his nose. "And during this," he said, "you saw Dad."

She nodded. "In the shed. It was like... the air lagged. Light lagged. Dust froze. Then he was there, between us and the bag. He pointed at my phone. It unlocked itself. The map app opened on its own. There were three pins and this line between them, like a triangle made of light. Places I knew—where stuff went off. Stairwell, café, that one street. And it was, like, humming. Then my head... I don't know. It felt like someone hit pause on me and play on something else. When I came back, he was gone. The map was normal. Mercedes said almost a minute."

She spoke faster at the end, like spitting it out before it spoiled.

Olle wrote while she talked, not missing a beat. He sketched a triangle, labelled each point with simple symbols instead of names. Then he looked up.

"Any sound?" he asked. "From him."

"No," she said. "Never."

"Any touch?"

She thought of the way the air felt thicker. "No. Just... more real than real. That's all."

He tapped the pencil on the $\Delta\tau$ **00:50** note. "Symptoms?"

"Nausea. Ringing ears. Metallic taste. My skull trying to exit my body." She hesitated. "Nosebleed."

"Which nostril?"

She stared at him. "Are you serious?"

"Yes."

"Left," she said.

He scribbled. "Okay."

"What does left mean?"

"We don't know yet," he said. "We collect. Then we decide."

She dropped back on his bed and covered her eyes with her forearm. "You sound like a cult."

"A data cult," he said. "It's the best kind."

Despite herself, a huff of almost-laughter escaped.

Silence stretched for a few seconds. Pencil on paper. The faint clink of a mug in the kitchen. Mandy's pulse in her ears.

Olle flipped to a clean page. At the top he wrote, in small, neat letters: **M**.

"Okay," he said. "What do we know for sure?"

"I hate this," she muttered.

"Number one," he went on, ignoring that, "you see Dad. Only you. Right?"

"Yeah." The word came out tight. "Just me."

"Number two. When you see him, time is wrong. For you." He tapped his pencil. "You blink and more has passed out here than in there."

"I... guess." She picked at a loose thread on his blanket. "In the shed, it felt like a blink. Mercedes says I was... off. Not answering. She was freaked."

"Call it a skip," Olle said. He wrote: **skip**. Underlined it. "Not a blackout, not sleep. A skip. Like your track jumped."

"It's not a track," Mandy said. "It's my brain."

"Your brain is a track," he said mildly. "Number three: headaches, ringing ears, metallic taste, nosebleed. That's new. Stronger."

"Is there a point to listing all the ways I'm broken?" she snapped.

He shook his head. "You're not broken. You're... reacting." He paused, searching for a word she wouldn't immediately flinch away from. "Something's interacting with you."

She made a face. "Wow. Thanks, Doctor Strange."

He held her gaze. "Mandy. If it was just in your head, it wouldn't steal time on the outside. Mercedes wouldn't see you freeze. The nosebleed's physical. So: something is touching your system from the outside."

"Like what? Ghost Wi-Fi?" she said, but more tired than mocking.

His mouth twitched. "Maybe. We don't know what. Yet. So we don't dress it up."

She blew out a breath. "Say it in a way I can understand please."

He tapped the pencil against the page, thinking. "Okay. Very small, non-scary version: Maybe he is trying to reach you from somewhere else."

"Somewhere else," she repeated. "Like from heaven?"

He shrugged one shoulder. "Could be dead, could be... different. Could be a place that's not here-here. I don't mean angels and harps. Just... not this system."

"How is 'place that's not this system' less scary?"

"It's more honest," he said. "And if he's reaching in, it costs something. Systems don't like being poked, so the cost is taken from the easiest place."

She knew before he said it.

"Me," she said.

He nodded once. "You're the contact point. So when he shows up, you pay. A little bit of your... time, present, *now,* whatever you want to call, it gets eaten."

Her stomach twisted. "Don't say it like that."

He crossed out "eaten" and wrote **used**. "Borrowed," he tried. "Just seconds. But fifty is a lot."

Mandy pressed her nails into her palms. "So every time I see him, I lose pieces of my life."

"Tiny ones," Olle said. "We don't know how stable it is. Or if it stacks. That's why I want to track it. If it's just this once, okay. If it keeps growing, we have a problem."

"We already have a problem," she whispered. "Bilal. The bag. All of it."

His eyes sharpened. "You still won't tell me exactly what happened."

"You don't want that," Mandy said quickly. "If you don't have the words, no one can pull them out of you. You know that, right?"

He hesitated, then gave a small nod. "Fine. Dangerous thing. He's using you. You hate it. That's enough for now."

She looked at him, surprised. "You're not going to yell at me?"

"If I yell, will it un-happen?" he asked.

"No."

"Then we save yelling for later," he said. "Right now: data."

"You're such a robot."

"Robots are efficient," he said. "Also fictional for now."

A reluctant smile ghosted across her face and vanished.

He turned the notebook so she could see the simple list:

1. Only Mandy sees Dad.

2. Time skips during appearances (outside time > inside).

3. Physical side effects (headache, ringing, nosebleed).

4. Appears during or near stress / danger.

5. Dad points — phone, map, numbers — like he's trying to show something.

"He's not random," Olle said softly. "He's... aiming."

"At what?" she asked.

"That's the part we don't know yet," he said. "Don't pretend we do."

"And the red numbers?" she added, the words shoved out before she lost courage. "Sometimes I see a countdown. On my screen. It flickers. I thought it was like... dream garbage. But it's the same style every time. Red. Digital. Ticking down from hours."

He wrote: **countdown?** with a question mark three times.

"Is it connected?" she asked.

"Maybe," he said. "Maybe not. Right now it's just another thing. If you see it again, try to remember the numbers if you can. Or screenshot if it's technically possible. We'll look for patterns. We're at the boring stage."

"Boring," she echoed. "Sure."

He studied her face again. "You have to tell me when it happens. Promise. No more skipping alone."

She shifted on the bed. "And if I don't?"

"I'll know," he said. "You get this... glassy look. Like Mercedes when she pretends she's not hungry."

Her head snapped up. "You noticed that?"

He went a bit red. "It's data," he muttered. "She eats more when Mom cooks. That means something."

"Oh my God," Mandy said slowly, a wicked edge breaking through the anxiety. "Do you have a crush on Mercedes?"

"No," he said too fast.

She raised an eyebrow.

He fussed with his pencil. "She's loud. And mean. And she smells like stolen perfume."

"That's not a no," Mandy said.

He scowled at his notebook. "...She's nice to you," he said quietly. "And she looks less sad here."

The answer softened her. "Then help me keep her alive," Mandy said.

His scowl shifted into something more focused. "I am," he said. "By making sure you don't fry your brain trying to watch ghost-TV alone."

She snorted. "Great. I'm premium cursed content."

"Exactly." He closed the notebook halfway. "Listen. We don't understand the rules yet. So: no heroic experiments. Don't try to trigger him. Don't stare at screens waiting. If he shows up, notice. Count, if you can. Then tell me."

"And if it gets worse?" she asked.

"Maybe we find someone smart who won't lock us up in an asylum."

"Like who?"

He hesitated, von Post's name almost visible on his tongue, then shook his head. "I don't know, adults complicate things."

"Understatement of the year," she muttered.

He slid the notebook fully closed; it felt like a promise. "For now it's just us," he said. "You, me. And Mercedes, of course. No Mom. No police."

"You're really swearing?" she said.

He looked up at her, suddenly very young and very serious. "On my graph pens," he said.

That landed heavier than it should. "Okay," she whispered. "On your graph pens."

She leaned over and bumped her forehead lightly against his. "Thanks, freak."

"Don't bleed on me," he said, but he didn't pull away.

She stood, hand already on the door handle, then paused. "Hey, Olle?"

"Mm?"

"If he is... trying to reach me from somewhere else," she said, softer, "do you think that means he's still... him?"

Olle considered. "I think," he said slowly, "nothing empty would bother. Whatever it is, it cares. That's enough for today."

It wasn't an answer, not really. It was something to hold.

She slipped out, closing the door with a careful click.

Olle sat for a long moment, staring at the closed notebook. Then he opened to the page with **M** again and added one last line:

Maybe: Dad reaching in = good. Time cost = bad. Watch both.

He underlined "watch both," circled the question marks around **countdown** once more, and turned off the lamp.

In the dark, the numbers he'd written seemed to float under his eyelids, rearranging themselves into possibilities he wasn't ready to say out loud. Not yet.

CHAPTER 10

Saturday tried to act like Saturday.

The sky did its best version of blue. A busker on Drottninggatan looped the same four chords and sang like he was auditioning for a life where smoke wasn't the first thing you smelled in the morning. Window displays put out their shiniest lies—dummies in denim laughing with no mouths; shoes arranged like stepping-stones into a future where you could afford them.

Mandy and Mercedes walked past it all with hands jammed into pockets that felt too shallow.

"Let's just... look," Mercedes said, the way you say *let's just breathe* to a person who's been holding their breath for a week. "Window shop. No stealing. Promise."

"Okay," Mandy said. Her voice didn't know how to be light today.

They did the circuit: Bianca's boutique (too loud to go in), the sneaker store with the wall that looked like a Tetris level, the little jewelry place where everything pretended to be gold and succeeded from far away. They paused in front of each glass, reflected back at themselves: two girls with hair done and eyeliner neat, faking ease. Inside, her body moved like a person walking through a museum where the exhibits were explosives.

Mercedes pressed her nose to a window, fogging a tiny circle. "Manifesting," she said, half teasing, half serious. "I manifest that bag." She pointed at a ridiculous leather thing that looked like it would squeal if it got wet.

"You can manifest your way into budgeting," Mandy said, automatic, the banter that kept the ground from opening under them.

Mercedes bumped her shoulder lightly. "You're no fun."

"I'm... tired," Mandy said. It came out smaller than she meant.

They drifted with the crowd, pretending to be current that belonged to this river. Two cops crossed the street behind them, not in a hurry, just... there, like potted plants with radios. A florist still had tape across one corner of the door where the glass had spidered weeks ago; today the tape was pink to look like a choice. A tram sighed by with half its seats empty because people had taught themselves to stand.

"Do you ever think about just... getting on a train and not getting off until it feels different?" Mercedes asked.

Mandy thought about the silos. The satchel. The message: *Good. You were quick.*

"Yeah," she said. "All the time."

They wound up near the café with the cracked window—the place that served coffee strong enough to clean a coin. It smelled like cinnamon and burnt sugar and safe. Inside, a student couple argued softly about something abstract and not life-threatening. Mandy wanted to sit down and borrow their problem for ten minutes.

They didn't go in.

They stood at the edge of the plaza, watching the big public clock do nothing dramatic. A crosswalk timer clicked down from 20, 19, 18, like a tutorial of how numbers are supposed to behave: politely, predictably.

Mercedes was talking—about a TikTok where a cat got its head stuck in a cereal box and the owner monologued like a therapist—when the air did that thing.

A soft shiver under the regular noise. The light around the edges of things thickened, like someone had added a clear syrup to the day. Sound slid farther away. Mandy recognized it now the way you recognize the start of a nosebleed or a panic attack: the warning with your name on it.

Her lungs forgot what to do for one half of a second.

Then he was there.

Her father stood to the left of the clock, not *really* there, but there enough that her heart did the jump and skid anyway. He wore the same jacket. His expression was the same—focused, apologetic, urgent, like he was late for a flight and the gate agent was her.

He lifted his hand and pointed. Not at the clock. At her phone, already in her palm because she'd been filming Mercedes's cat-story eyes.

The screen woke without her touch. The red digital numbers pulsed up—bold, impersonal: **62:00:00**, and then peeled down with a smooth hiss to **61:59:59**. Beside it, for a blink, the map overlayed itself: three nodes flared like pushpins on fire. The line between them traced into a triangle. At its center, something ghosted, a softer light where no pin yet lived.

Her father's fingertip followed the triangle's legs, steady, once, twice, like he was teaching a child to write. His face flickered in and out of the glass reflection. He made a small motion, *watch*, and then pointed again, hard, at the center.

Her stomach dropped like a floor wasn't where it was supposed to be.

"—hello? Mandy?" Mercedes's voice sounded like it was coming through a fan.

Mandy tried to breathe. Her vision tunneled, expanded, tunneled again. The red numbers stuttered—**61:59:41, …39, …38**—and then the entire screen went not-black but *blank*, like someone had wiped it. Her father held, held—

—and let go.

The day snapped back, too bright. All the sound rushed into her ears at once. The clock on the building had skipped two minutes. Her knees didn't ask permission. They gave out. The last thing she saw before the pavement rose was Mercedes's mouth shaping *no*.

∧∨∧

She came back to herself the way you come up from too deep in a pool: pressure first, then sound, then color. Someone had turned the world down to a hum. She lay flat on a bench with her head in Mercedes's lap, a crumpled napkin wedged awkwardly under her nose. The napkin tasted like coffee and paper dust.

"Hi," Mercedes said, like people say to babies that just scared everyone. "Do that again and I will literally kill you."

"Noted," Mandy said. The word was a croak.

"Drink," Mercedes ordered, shoving a water bottle into her hands.

Mandy sat up slow. The plaza did a small spin and calmed down. No one was filming, thank God. Two aunties pretended not to stare. The cops two corners back had not moved; if they had noticed at all, they had classified *fainting teenage girl* as Not Our Department.

"How long?" Mandy asked, throat tight.

"Two minutes and... a bit," Mercedes said. Her hand was on Mandy's shoulder like she was keeping gravity from misplacing her again. "I thought you died."

"Sorry," Mandy said, because it was what you said, and because it fit everything. She dabbed at her nose. Pink on white. Not dramatic. Proof anyway.

Mercedes leaned closer. "Was it him?" she asked, voice tiny around the edges.

Mandy nodded. She swallowed down the tremor. "The numbers. The map. The... triangle again. And something in the middle. Like a not-pin. He wanted me to see it."

Mercedes's eyes flashed frustration at a universe that would use a dead father as a user interface. "I hate this," she said.

"Me too," Mandy said. They sat there a long minute, breathing and letting the world be world-shaped.

"Tell Olle," Mercedes said finally. "Please. Before I start googling *'my best friend is glitching, is she a robot'.*"

Mandy barked out a laugh she didn't recognize. "Okay."

They got up slow. Mercedes looped an arm under Mandy's and walked her the way you walk someone you love who isn't good at asking for help. They didn't go home. Home was a place where mothers asked *what happened* and where the answer could not be said out loud. They walked two blocks, then another, returned to the tram. The tune the busker played had changed; it was still the same four chords.

On the ride, Mandy texted with thumbs that still felt like borrowed equipment.

Mandy → Olle: *It happened again. Longer. Two minutes? Map + triangle + center. Nosebleed, fainted. Do NOT tell mom.*

The typing bubble appeared so fast she pictured him already hunched over his desk, as if he'd never left.

Olle: *Are you okay.*
Mandy: *Functional.*
Olle: *I think I maybe suspect something. Need time. Come home slowly and tell me any numbers you remember, I'll log it.*
Mandy: *Slowly is my only speed right now.*

Olle: *Drink salty thing. Pressure helps.*
Mandy: *Ew.*
Olle: *Science.*
Mandy: *Okay, Science.*

∧∨∧

Night stretched out like old gum. It didn't snap; it just got thinner and stickier and everywhere. Mandy lay on her side, watching the silhouette of her plant do nothing important. Every time she closed her eyes, the red numbers pulsed the inside of her lids. When she did drift, a door slammed in another apartment and she came up choking on adrenaline like she'd been underwater again.

Through the wall, Olle's lamp stayed on. Paper whispered. Once, a chair creaked like a ship. He coughed. He did not sleep. She hated and loved him for it.

At some point, she padded out for water. In the kitchen, the clock read 02:11. Olle stood there already, in his hoodie, like a raccoon that had evolved thumbs and spreadsheets.

"Go back to bed," she said.

He didn't look up from the notebook open on the counter. "I can't," he said simply. Then, "Here." He slid over a small plate: two crackers, a handful of salted peanuts.

She raised an eyebrow.

"Pressure," he said. "Salt. To keep your blood happy."

"You made that up." She ate it anyway. The peanuts felt like something a human would do.

"Any ideas?" she asked, careful.

He lifted one shoulder. "I need to check something in the morning. Not Google-level, street-level."

"Olle," she said, warning and affection braided together.

"I won't tell anyone," he said. "I just need the library maps."

"Okay." she muttered. "But if you get arrested for being a nerd, I'm not bailing you out."

"You can't," he said. "We don't have bail money."

She snorted. He allowed himself a small smile. They stood there a minute in the weird peace of kitchens at two a.m.

"Try and sleep," he said finally.

"I'll practice fainting," she deadpanned.

He shot her a look. She went back to bed, exhausted and electrically awake. She slept twenty minutes, badly. The red numbers waited at the end of every fourteen-blink run.

∧∨∧

Mandy's door burst open at 07:12, taking years off her life.

"Olle—"

"Don't yell," he said, already hauling a roll of printed maps out of his armpit and elbowing her desk clear with a sweep of his forearm. "Also, get up."

"I was— I hate you," she said fondly, pushing hair from her face and sitting up. The room smelled like paper and pencil lead, a kind of church.

He taped the first map down with washi tape stolen from some forgotten craft kit. City grid. Major streets and transit lines. Then another layer: colored transparency with power infrastructure, thin veins of cable converging on thicker trunks. A third: water mains. A fourth: the sites of recent blasts, marked with neat red dots and thin dates in his tiny script.

"Since when do we own a plotter?" she asked.

"Library," he said. "And the internet. And a printer with no shame." He pinned three corners with textbooks. His hands shook a little: not with fear or coffee, but with the excitement of numbers deciding to behave.

"Okay," he said, breathless. "Don't... try to keep up."

"What."

"I don't think the countdown is a clock," he said.

She frowned. "What is a countdown if not a clock?"

NODE ZERO

"Codes can look like clocks," he said, tapping at the red dots. "Phone number strings look like dates. Humans see patterns where we want them. You saw red numbers next to a map. Your brain said 'timer.' But what if those numbers are labels? A way to index locations. Or to mark a sequence that isn't about time, but *order.*"

She tugged the blanket tighter around her shoulders. "Olle, use human words."

He pointed at the three nearest red dots. "The triangle you saw? If you draw lines between certain numbers you saw on the city grid... look."

He'd already drawn it. The triangle sat there on paper like it had been waiting for them.

"At the center," he went on, stabbing a pencil at the interior, "won't be a coffee shop or a bench or a place normal people care about. It's—" he slid the power-lines transparency over the map again; the thin lines crossed, then merged into a fat knot right where his pencil rested, "—a substation nexus. Old. Busy. Everything passes through it."

"Power," Mandy murmured, feeling the weight of that word in a new way. Not just light-switches. Windows you couldn't see.

"Node," he said. "Call it Node Zero for us. The center of that triangle can be the exact place where the city's electrical guts are thinnest and most... *converged.*" He looked up to make sure she was coming with him. "If someone wanted to... do something that needed a lot of energy and a little bit of geometry, they'd aim for there."

Her mouth had gone dry. "Do what?"

"I don't know," he said, honest. "That's the piece I don't have. *Yet.* But you said Dad didn't point at random. He pointed at that center. Twice. First in the shed, then yesterday."

She rubbed at the sore spot on her upper lip where the napkin had chafed. "You said the countdown's not a timer."

He nodded, hair flopping into his eyes and not being brushed away because both hands were busy with the world. "Those numbers could be node IDs. Or sequence steps for... events at different places that add up to something at the center. Like—

" he swallowed, groping for an image she'd accept— "like three people pressing buttons at the corners of a triangle to unlock a door in the middle. Not time. Coordination."

She stared at the lines. The red triangle sat there like a trap someone else had laid around a thing they wanted.

"What about the losing-time bit," she asked. "The... *me* part."

He flicked eyes to her, worried. "That part I still think is him trying to reach you. From... somewhere else. We don't know the where. And every time he does, you pay seconds. Yesterday you paid about one-twenty. That's... a lot, considering your body goes catatonic while being in a space that's not entirely of this world." He dug in his hoodie pocket and pulled out a tiny spiral-bound notepad, the cheap kind detectives use in shows. On the front, in his neat block letters: **Δτ LOG**. He grimaced at her expression. "Don't freak out."

"I'm not," she lied.

"I need to know if it's getting worse," he said gently. "If it's linear or exponential. If... If anything helps. Because if we can't stop the appearances, we can only try to limit the damage." He touched the base of her skull lightly with two fingers, tentative. "It's your brain. I don't want it... frayed."

She fought down a sweep of gratitude sharp enough to hurt. "I'll try to... not be reachable," she said weakly.

"That's not how it works," he said. "It's not you calling him. It's him calling you." He hesitated, then added, "I think."

"And the numbers," she said, reaching for something she could stand on. "If they're labels... how do we use them?"

He chewed the inside of his cheek. "We collect enough to map. If we can get more, we can predict the exact locations and its center. If the pattern holds. And if there are more dots—" he tapped a cluster further out on the map with a pencil eraser, places she recognized from headlines and tape— "we see if they make other shapes. If they point to other centers."

She tried to picture her father in another place with a different sky, looking at a map like this and deciding what to draw for her with limited ink. The thought made her both brave and nauseous.

"So what do we do," she asked. "Right now?"

He huffed a breath. "Right now, you try not to faint in public again."

"Copy that."

"You keep your phone on you but don't stare at it," he said. "If you feel it coming, sit. Breathe. Count out loud if you can. Give me the numbers if the red thing shows up. I'll write them. Ask Mercedes to do the same. Just—say what you see."

"Okay," she said. It felt like agreeing to be a lab rat with agency.

"And no adults," he added, eyes flicking briefly toward the door, where their mother's voice drifted in from the radio. "Not yet."

"Agreed," she said immediately.

He lingered, hand still on the power-lines overlay like he couldn't bear to let go of the only solid thing. "I don't know if he's from... there," he said softly, not looking at her. "The parallel thing. I just think it's not here. And I think he thinks Node Zero matters." He swallowed. "I think he's scared."

The word made something inside her tip. Her father, scared. "Then we listen," she said. She reached out and flattened her palm over the center of the triangle. The paper was cool. The pencil dent under her hand felt like a pulse. "We figure out what *here* is supposed to do with this."

Mandy exhaled, long. She lay back and held her phone over her head, watching the lock screen do nothing sinister. She wanted to throw it into the ocean. She wanted to tape it to her chest like a beacon. She pressed the side button and turned it dark and placed it face down.

In the quiet, she could almost hear the red numbers breathing on the other side of the glass. Not *tick*, exactly. Not *time*. More like *places* waiting their turn. A geometry someone else had started, counting not down but *in*. Toward a center.

CHAPTER 11

Aldina started with the hardware because hardware never lied on purpose.

On the stainless table in the lab she'd hijacked for the afternoon, three clock modules sat in a neat row, each bagged and tagged from different "minor" incidents: a stairwell blast that singed paint, a café door that blew outward instead of inward (odd), and a trash-can pop that did more to scare pigeons than people. She'd pulled the timers apart so many times her fingers remembered the pattern. Same board layout. Same cheap oscillator. Same EEPROM image, hex dump identical to the byte. No radio, no GSM, no RF antenna stubs, nothing that would take a command from a distance. All local-arm, all on the same absurdly fussy timebase.

If you wanted maximum carnage, this wasn't what you built.

If you wanted *predictable, repeatable micro-events* at *predictable places*, it was exactly what you built.

She lifted the café timer and turned it. Even the solder beads were in the same places, like the person assembling them had jigged themselves into the job. She glanced at the note she'd written in the margin of her own report that morning, **IDENTICAL FIRMWARE/NO REMOTE CAPABILITY**, then struck a line through the "NO" and wrote → **PURPOSELY NONE**. There was a difference between what something couldn't do and what someone had *chosen* not to let it do.

The prints came back clean. Of course they did. When they didn't, they came back muddled, shared across half a dozen low-level runners who would swear their way into "transferable DNA" acquittals while prosecutors fumed. The *pattern* wasn't on fingers.

It was in the grid.

She rolled the wall map down in her apartment that night, tape crackling as it stuck and re-stuck to the plaster. Red dots for blast sites. Thin pencil dates. She took a ruler and pretended she wasn't taking a ruler, then lightly connected the last three.

36: 200
25: 100
50: 500
320: 001
19: 126
10: 500
25: 002
1: 100
102: 100
22: 102
129: 00
92: 100
142: 100

A triangle blinked at her from the mess of streets. She added the two sets from the previous fortnight. Another triangle, offset and rotated, sharing one leg. She stacked transparencies, one for power infrastructure (hard to get, but she'd needed only one engineer at City Grid AB to hate his boss and believe in texts from an unknown number that said "coffee?"), one for telecom trunk routes, one for water mains.

Power told the story.

Every triangle she drew wrapped a substation or an older switching yard, sometimes both. Not on the dot, never that obvious, but like a bow tied around a gift. And every time the third corner hit, the incident report log she'd pulled from the dispatch system showed a brief brownout or a protection trip five to nine minutes later, logged by a sleepy technician with "INVESTIGATE" carried forward to the next shift, then again to the next.

She stared at the wall until the clusters stopped being dots and started being *choices*.

Choice meant a person.

Choice meant intent.

Her phone buzzed on the kitchen counter. Two messages from a detective she'd stopped returning calls from because he worked the old way and she didn't have patience for old. *"You're not on these any more, Aldina."* She flipped the phone face down and went back to the threads. The old way hadn't saved her father. The old way closed a case on a hard-earned criminal due to technicalities and called it done.

Three hours into the night, she had what she needed to feel right in her bones: a hypothesis that kept refusing to be wrong when she poked it.

Whoever placed these devices wasn't trying to terrorize random coffee drinkers. They were *stimulating* points on the grid, small transient spikes that would ripple inward. If you believed the engineer she'd bought soup for at lunch (and she did), stations will ride through a few such events without blinking; but the old ones, the ones with parts sourced from the era when you could smoke at your desk, they'd cough. They'd shed load. They'd reveal their weak welds and sticky breakers.

Someone was probing. Someone with a map that wasn't the public one.

She needed something more to go with it.

∧∨∧

Access was a personality test.

On paper, she didn't have the authority to request financials outside the narrow bounds of a specific case. In practice, she was very good at asking for things as if she'd already been granted them, then making it hard for the recipient to admit they'd let a rule be more important than a result. She drafted three emails that read like continuations of conversations that hadn't happened yet, attached a "pre-approved" routing memo (unsigned; most people didn't look for signatures in the first pass), CC'd one bored prosecutor who owed her a favor, and sent them to: a mid-level analyst in Financial Crimes with a reputation for being too strict to be popular; an anti-money-laundering investigator at a bank where half of Sable Line's relatives parked their weekend cash; and a municipal contracts officer who posted process memes on LinkedIn and therefore would not want to look like the sort of person who *didn't* cooperate.

She set a timer for forty minutes, drank bad coffee while the timer droned, then did what she always did when she needed to feel the world again: she opened the folder with the bus stop photos. Her father's route. What a "minor device" did when a man stood too close on the wrong day because the clouds promised rain.

She flipped it closed before the timer finished. The photos didn't help her work; they helped her remember *why* she was willing to be the sort of person who put a thumb on the scale.

Replies came in like rain starting, one drop, then three at once.

Financial Crimes could provide sanitized Suspicious Transaction Reports where Sable Line–adjacent entities were mentioned; the analyst could not promise names, but she could promise patterns. The bank investigator, to her surprise, offered a call: *"Off the record, but I'm tired of filing forms into a shredder."* The contracts officer sent a link to the public procurement portal with a flair of passive aggression, *"As you surely know, these are all open as a matter of course"*, and, significantly, a CSV of recent "risk consultancy" vendor awards that had not yet been posted publicly.

Aldina smiled without humor. People always told you who they were if you gave them a chance.

She put the CSV on the map.

Two vendor names came up again and again over the last nine months: **Northbridge Risk AB** and **LinjAnalytik Konsult HB**. They didn't smell like real companies; they smelled like brand kits thrown together in an afternoon by someone who'd watched an American show about Swedish corporate names. The awards were small enough to not draw press, 200,000 SEK here for "grid resilience modeling," 350,000 SEK there for "transient response consultation," often split across departments, Public Utilities, Emergency Preparedness, even Cultural Venues where old theaters still used the city's lines like life support.

Northbridge invoiced for "testing advisories." LinjAnalytik billed for "risk models."

She swore softly at her wall. The triangle was not a coincidence. It was a memo.

She pulled Northbridge in the business registry. The directors you could see were a kindergarten of straw men: a dead-eyed twenty-one-year-old who "lived" at five different apartments on paper; a woman who moved between cleaning jobs and had a signature that didn't match the one on her social posts; an Estonian holding company with a postbox as a heart. The beneficial owners field was a desert.

She climbed LinjAnalytik. Same sandpit. The address pointed to a co-working space that had changed names three times and featured aspirational photos of people high-fiving.

She took the bank investigator's call on her balcony with the wind slicing off the water and the city lights pretending to be stars. He didn't give his name.

"You didn't get this from me," he said without hello. "But the same merchant IDs that receive payments for those consultancies disburse cash to several accounts clustered around a laundry of Sable Line businesses. Shisha lounges, a car wash in Kista that runs mostly at 2 a.m., a courier service that never files mileage. The flows are sideways. In on one entity, out to five, back again by Friday."

"Kickbacks?" she asked.

"Or funding," he said. "The tags on the payments say 'equipment,' 'professional services,' 'incident review'." A pause. "I will say: every time you folks log an 'incident' that makes the news, my STR queue lights up the next day with micro-transfers bouncing through those shells. It looks like somebody paying out bonuses. Or settling invoices."

"Same beneficiary?"

Silence hummed. "The beneficiaries are masked," he said. "But the final hop before it goes dark is a *risk consultancy* with a different name every quarter. New bank, new number, same merchant descriptor string. The narrative attached to the bank file says 'embedded project advisor for city power upgrades.'"

"Inside actor," she said. It wasn't a question.

"You didn't hear anything from me."

"I didn't," she said, and meant it.

After she hung up, she stared so hard at **Northbridge Risk AB** that the letters blurred and reassembled themselves. *North*, as in orienting. *Bridge*, as in spanning. It was childish to assign symbolism to shells, but she let herself have the thought and wrote it down in small letters anyway.

Then she printed three invoices she had no right to have: Northbridge to Public Utilities, advisory hours annotated with consultant initials; LinjAnalytik to the same, "triangulation risk" annotated with terse bullet points; and a third, newer entity, **Post-Strata Advisory**, billing under the umbrella of "Substation Modernization: Phase 2".

She circled the third name, held the page at arm's length. She flipped to the second page. Consultant initials appeared in the margins like you'd leave crumbs to your future self: **KVP, A.R., LinA**. She underlined them all twice, wrote **find, don't guess** next to it, and moved on. Names behind shells had a way of surfacing if you put the right questions in the right ears.

∧∨∧

The mall made normal into architecture.

Saturday afternoon crowds slipped along escalators like oil. Scent machines kept mint hovering where sweat would be. A cello cover of some pop song echoed up the atrium, turning human into soundtrack. The lights were bright and discreet, the kind that made your skin look more alive than you felt.

"Again," Mercedes said, sotto voce, as they approached the glass doors. "We're just... us. Looking. Slow feet. No tugging."

"Don't teach me how to be a teenage girl," Mandy said, because the alternative was saying *I'm scared.* She checked her reflection once in a chrome pillar—not the vanity check, the *do I look like a person who can pass* check—and followed Mercedes in.

They did a loop the way you pretend to do loops: not quite aimless. Up the wide stairs, pause at the railing for the view down into the fountain, turn left at the bookstore as if drawn to a display of cookbooks no one their age bought. Past cosmetics (linger for a wrist spritz), past athleisure (snort at a pair of leggings that cost as much as rent), then into the cluster of little shops near the back where, yesterday, a rent-a-cop had told a boy with a hoodie to take his hood down in a voice that tried not to sound like a dare.

Mercedes narrated under her breath. "If we get spooked, you peel into that tea place. I go through the jeans store and out the service door. Meet at the back stairs. If back stairs blocked, we take the elevator like we're late. Never run. Running is an announcement."

"Running announces, right," Mandy repeated, trying to make her body memorize what her head knew.

They walked the potential drop route without the thing they might be carrying, letting muscle build a map. The alley outside the west exit—that was where the text had told them the stash would go eventually. Mandy counted bread-crumbs: missing tile near the smoothie kiosk, squeaky spot just before the jeweler where you had to control your face.

He was there. Of course he was.

Bilal didn't follow them like a creep. He didn't need to. He appeared three times, not close, never too far, once reflected in a sunglasses rack, once leaned against a column scrolling his phone, once riding the escalator opposite them, descending as they ascended, his gaze flicking off them and back as if they were just two more things he was inventorying. No swagger. No look-at-me. A stillness you learned from standing watch for long hours in places where sitting got you yelled at.

Mercedes clocked him first and pretended not to have clocked him. Her shoulder set. Her spine lengthened. The tiny hard thing in her eyes, the one that said *don't you dare hurt me and don't you dare stop looking at me* flickered on and off.

At the second pass, he cut diagonally across their path in the broad walkway where the ceiling turned higher and the light turned expensive. He didn't touch them. He didn't even slow. He murmured it like the sentence had someplace else to be: "Don't rehearse fear."

Mandy's mouth went dry. "We're not rehearsing anything," she said, without looking at him.

"Rehearse the walk out," he said. "Not the panic."

"We're multitasking," Mercedes said.

His left eyebrow twitched. Approval? Annoyance? Both? "If something tips," he said, "you are two girls going to pretzel place. You are arguing about cinnamon versus salt. You are not heroes."

"Stop saying that word," Mercedes said. "It makes people want to prove you wrong."

He didn't smile. He didn't leave a threat. He merged into a family of four with matching puffer jackets and vanished down the escalator as if he belonged to them. Mandy felt a weird twist of relief and bile: the way he could disappear made her both safer and more in danger.

They finished the loop. Twice. By the third pass Mandy felt her legs learning which pace read as "window shopping" and which read as "mission." She kept catching herself checking the digital clock above the cinema—the habit now of watching numbers for betrayal.

"Pretzels?" Mercedes asked finally, as if to bless the practice with something actually edible.

"Cinnamon," Mandy said, and they stood in line and did the banal thing with an intensity that would have been funny yesterday. Behind them, a couple argued softly about whether to buy a blender. In the reflection of the pretzel case, a hood went by that *might* have been Bilal's and also might have been a stranger who didn't know any of their names.

They ate the pretzel outside on the bench where a potted plant did its best to be a tree. They didn't talk about the satchel that wasn't yet theirs or the alley that would be. They talked about the cello cover song and whether it made you a better person to play sad songs in major key.

When they left, they took the back stairs, because it was important that their feet know how those stairs felt. Mercedes counted steps under her breath in fours. Mandy ran her hand along the rail to memorize the cold.

Outside, the day had gone gray. A woman passed with a stroller and a coffee she'd earned. A delivery truck idled with a rattle like a smoker's cough. The alley that would eventually matter looked like all alleys look until they don't.

"Again tomorrow?" Mercedes said, as if it were a normal plan about fries and a movie.

"Again tomorrow," Mandy said.

CHAPTER 12

Mandy rehearsed the speech all the way up the science wing stairs and forgot every word the second she saw Kim von Post's door.

The placard read PHYSICS in dull letters, and someone—probably last year's jokers—had stuck a tiny dinosaur sticker under the P, like time had misfiled one creature here and nobody bothered to peel it off. Inside, the lab had the kind of order that looked accidental until you tried to move anything: coils nested in labeled trays, a stack of battered journals with bookmarks like shy tongues, a whiteboard dense with symbols but tidy margins, as if the math believed in public manners.

Von Post herself was at the desk, glasses higher on her head than her eyes, blue hair soft today instead of spiked, like she had three versions of herself and this was the one for anxious students. She looked up when Mandy hovered in the doorway and did the small welcoming gesture that always worked—the palm lifted a few centimeters, the almost-smile, the "you're not interrupting anything even if you are."

"Hey," Mandy said, then hated how small the word sounded in her own mouth.

"Hi, Mandy." Von Post pushed the glasses down where they belonged and angled her chair so it was half to the desk, half to Mandy. "You look as if you're either about to cry or about to ask a good question. Both are science."

A laugh escaped Mandy before she could stop it. That was the dangerous part about Kim: she diffused everything with a tone that made you want to hand her the bomb just to get rid of it.

"I... can I... It's weird," she said. "It *will* sound weird."

"Good," von Post said lightly. "Weird is an early form of correct."

Mandy stepped in and shut the door behind her without being asked. The blinds were up, the winter daylight thin and honest. She didn't sit right away; she pressed her fingers into the edge of a lab table like the wood could keep her from floating.

"I've been having... glitches," she said, loading the word with air quotes even though she didn't lift her hands. "I see... something. Like an overlay. On my phone, but not *on* my phone. Big red numbers. Counting down. Or like coordinates? Or so my brother thinks. And then—" she swallowed, and the swallow hurt, like the truth had angles— "my dad." She watched for the flinch, the teacher face, the pity. She saw neither. "He... shows up. Not... not *actually*, I know that. Like an image. He points. At the phone. At a map. And then I lose time." The last bit fell out in a rush. "Like a minute. Sometimes less. The hallway clock jumps forward. I get a nosebleed. And my head—" she made a fist and tapped her temple twice— "bangs."

Von Post's eyes went still. Not blank; focused. A lens adjusting, then holding. When she spoke, her voice dropped into the register people used at hospital bedsides and after nightmares.

"You've had a medical check recently?" she asked first. "Headaches can have boring causes. Low iron. Dehydration. Not enough sleep." A pause. "Trauma."

"Dehydration, probably," Mandy said, even though she knew she drank water like it was a sport. "And... grief. I guess."

"Grief is physics that happens inside you," von Post said. "It can bend time just by sitting there."

Mandy breathed. The room's hum—faint electronics, the distant cough of a vent—flattened out, less menacing.

"Tell me about the map," von Post said, casual, softly curious, as if the map were a bug Mandy had found on the windowsill. "What does it show?"

"A triangle," Mandy said before she could choose not to. "Three points. Places where... there were... I don't know... some kind of power lines, or so Olle said. When I saw it, it felt like... like it was telling me something. Go here, don't go here, I can't tell."

"And the countdown?" von Post asked. The light shifted on her glasses and Mandy could see her own small reflection in the lens. "Numbers that... jump?"

"They jump," Mandy said. "Like—" She fumbled for the words. "Like it counts, then it... leaps. Like it's on a different clock that sometimes decides to sync and sometimes gets bored and wanders off." She managed a tight half-smile. "I know it sounds insane."

"It sounds like noise riding signal," von Post said, and for a moment her voice went just a little too bright—hunger dressed as interest—before smoothing into teacher-tone again. "When did it last show up?"

"Yesterday evening," she said, trying to make her tone unhelpful. "Around ten."

"Mmm." Von Post nodded once, as if she'd input a value into an equation on the fly. "Does it always happen at night?"

"No," Mandy said, and instantly wished she'd said yes, because *yes* made it smaller and wronger and less relevant to anything that would interest adults who might take matters out of her hands.

"Okay." Von Post leaned back, and the chair made a sound like an old boat. "A few things." She held up fingers and counted them, slow, as if even the counting was meant to calm. "First, you're not crazy. Second, the human brain is a liar. Third, if you were my research subject, I would want three kinds of data: *when* you see the overlays or the numbers, *what* you see, and *how your body reacts*. That's as simple as a diary. Each entry: timestamp, location, what appeared, duration if you can guess, and symptoms—headache, nosebleed, blackout length."

Mandy nodded before she could stop herself. It's the same thing Olle had said, so maybe they were already on the right track.

"Hydrate," von Post continued. "Eat protein before school. Don't skip sleep for TikTok. Carry tissues." Her mouth flicked, almost a smile. "And if you ever feel there is a *pattern*—if the triangles repeat or the numbers correlate with anything you can name—bring it to me. We'll look without... judgment."

Mandy felt the room tip gently, like an elevator starting up. She kept nodding because nodding was easier than saying anything else.

"Are you safe?" Kim asked then, right in the center of Mandy's chest. Different question, different tone. "Not philosophically. Physically. Do you feel endangered?"

Mandy's heartbeat changed its coat. "I— No," she said. "Not directly. It's just in my head."

"Everything is in your head," von Post said, and the softness returned. "But that doesn't mean it is not true. Go to class. Drink water. Begin a diary. We can only outsmart a thing we can name."

Mandy stood. The chair legs made a little scrape and she winced like she'd knocked over a beaker. As she turned, Kim spoke one more time, almost as if to the air rather than to her.

"If you notice any *change*," she said, "even small—text me, or come to the lab. It matters."

Mandy left with a sensation that she had just fed a small, quick animal from her palm and it had licked her fingers with a tongue that was too warm.

In the hallway, Mercedes leaned against the lockers like a question mark drawn in lipstick.

"Where'd you go?" she asked. "You vanished after chem. I was about to set a flare."

"Bathroom," Mandy said, and Mercedes gave her the face you gave liars you loved.

"Fine," Mercedes said. "Bathroom that takes twenty-three minutes. You okay?"

Mandy nodded like a bobblehead. "Yeah. Just needed... air."

"Gross school air," Mercedes said, linking their arms automatically, a reflex as old as seventh grade. "Come. I found a meme that will either heal your soul or make you bite someone."

"Both are science," Mandy murmured, and when Mercedes peered at her, she shook her head. "I'll tell you later."

"After we don't die," Mercedes said, not quite joking.

"After we don't die," Mandy echoed.

∧∨∧

The message from the unknown number came mid-afternoon, when the day had folded into the kind of gray that made windows reflect more school than sky.

At 18:40, Mandy's phone buzzed with a number she didn't recognize and a text that felt like a hand placed, very lightly, on her shoulder.

Unknown:
Meet me where the bridge shadows hit the graffiti at 19:30. Alone for five minutes. Then bring your friend.

Mandy stared until the letters blended. *Not Bilal.* The tone was wrong. It had grammar. It had patience. It had the smell of police and the posture of someone who didn't trust police enough to admit it.

"Spam?" Mercedes asked, peering.

"Different," Mandy said. Her stomach remembered the alley. The flower pot. The way fear rearranged your organs and then asked you to run.

"I hate different," Mercedes said, then looked again. "We are not doing *alone*, babe."

Mandy's thumb hovered. She typed *who is this* and deleted it. She typed *no* and deleted that too. She sent a single dot, because a dot was nothing and everything, a pin on a map waiting to be labeled.

The reply came back with a picture: the underside of the footbridge by the canal at dusk, the triangle tag you could only see if you knew how to look—in chalk, not spray paint, so it washed when it rained. Someone had drawn a thin circle around it, like a teacher grading.

Unknown:
Five minutes. Then both. If I wanted you hurt, I'd pick easier places.

"Who the hell," Mercedes whispered, "texts like Batman?"

"Someone who could maybe save our Gotham?" Mandy said.

"I hate being wrong," Mercedes muttered. "We go. We leave in five if you tell your mom we're at mine."

"Done," Mandy said. "And you tell yours you're... wherever she won't check."

"Done," Mercedes said, and didn't smile.

∧∨∧

The bridge undersides always smelled the same: cold water, stale beer, kid courage. They got there early enough to watch the day exhale its last real light, then changed angles twice to ensure nobody waited behind the pillar they didn't check first. Mandy felt like she had eyes in the back of her neck and no lids for any of them. She kept her hands out, visible, the way people in movies did when they wanted to show they weren't carrying anything but a desperate wish to go home alive.

The woman stepped out of the shadow like she'd been made there.

Leather jacket, cheap sneakers that looked fast, hair pulled tight in a way that read either discipline or a headache. She kept her palms visible too, which didn't mean she was harmless. The face was familiar without being known: the face of someone you'd see on a tram and then remember later only as an impression of cheekbones and attention. When she spoke, the voice had the dry rasp of a throat that didn't love coffee but drank it anyway because sleep did not respect her.

"I'm Aldina," she said. She didn't add a last name and didn't offer a badge. "I work... not exactly where you think, but near enough. I know you've been involved by a man—or more like a young boy-- who goes by Bilal. He is not the top of anything. He is the face that gets punched while the hand hides."

Mandy's heart did the drum again. Mercedes slid half a step in front of her without making theater of it.

"We don't know any—" Mercedes began.

"Please," Aldina said, and the word was not a command; it was an exhausted idea. "You can call me a liar later. For the next minute, listen and then decide if you want to tell me to leave you alone forever."

Mandy didn't nod. She didn't breathe. She waited.

"I know," Aldina said, "someone is using boys like him to place devices in a pattern that has nothing to do with scaring people in cafés." She flicked her eyes to the chalk triangle as if to apologize for how much she didn't want to explain in a place where sound carried. "I think those devices are more about power than fear. And I know—" she tapped her phone, which remained in her pocket— "that nothing you do will save you from escaping their clutches."

"Have you been watching us?" Mercedes said. Her voice had shards in it. "That's creepy."

"I've been watching him," Aldina said. "You are the collateral. I don't like collateral."

"Then stop him," Mercedes snapped.

"That's the plan," Aldina said. "My way requires you to do nothing that will get you killed."

"Great plan," Mercedes said. "We love not dying."

Aldina's mouth did not quite curve, but her eyes softened by a millimeter. "I know you have a bag pickup coming," she continued. "Probably soon. You will be asked to carry it to a drop location." She lifted a hand when Mercedes sucked in a breath to swear. "You will do what he asks," she said, and Mercedes did swear then, quiet and bitter, because the words felt like betrayal. "And then, when he looks away, you will *buy us time.* I will be there. We will make the bag not do what it was built to do."

"You want us to carry a bomb," Mercedes said flatly.

"I want you to make a decision before someone else writes your names on a list that hurts me to look at," Aldina said, and finally the heat showed through the careful. "I want you to *pretend* to do what he says and then do the thing that lets me take him off the board and to whoever is pulling his strings."

Mandy measured the woman in front of her the way you measure a rope before you decide to climb it. "And after?" she asked. "He has... he has people."

"Yes," Aldina said. "And I will go for the ones above him too." The sentence sounded like a promise she'd carved into her ribs and then bandaged. "I will keep you girls *safe,*" she said softly.

Mandy looked at Mercedes. Mercedes looked at Mandy. The look held a decade: playgrounds, slammed lockers, everything they'd stolen that nobody missed, everything they'd lost on schedule.

"No delivery," Mandy said softly, and understood that she had just chosen a side. "We clock him. We steal time."

"We steal time," Mercedes echoed, and the phrase felt like anger wearing a new dress.

"Good," Aldina said. "Text this number." She recited it. "Do not save it under my name. Save it under something boring, like *Dentist*. And..." She hesitated, then added the sentence that made her shoulders heavier. "If he or any of the other guys touch you, scream like you want the world to end and I will make that noise true for him."

Mandy's throat burned. She nodded, and anything that might have been tears chose a different woman to bother tonight. Mercedes exhaled a laugh that wasn't one.

"Okay, Batman," she said. "We'll go to the bridge with the boy who thinks he is a bridge."

"Good," Aldina said, and the corner of her mouth admitted it wanted to be a smile someday.

She stepped backward into the shadow and became a shape, then a suggestion, then the fact that someone had been there who made the air different.

"Is this bad that I like her?" Mercedes whispered.

"It is consistent," Mandy said.

"With what?"

"With us liking the wrong things," Mandy said, and they both snorted softly, then straightened, already anxious of what is ahead.

CHAPTER 13

The message didn't come like the others. No clipped instructions. No emojis, no threats shaped like courtesy. It was a single-call buzz that vibrated straight through Mandy's palm and left her skin feeling misfiled.

Unknown:
Change in plans. Drop to be earlier. Meet me now. Same yard. Come alone to the road under the cranes. No phones out.

Mandy stared until the words stopped being words and became a problem. The clock on her lock screen said 18:11. The city outside the window felt... tilted, as if the day had been very slightly pried up at one edge. She could hear the hum of traffic, but it was the wrong pitch, the way a song sounds when the person playing it uses the wrong key and pretends you won't notice.

She found Mercedes already halfway into her boots, hair jammed into a messy knot that said *speed over pretty*.

"He moved it," Mandy said. "Earlier."

Mercedes's mouth pressed flat. "Of course he did. Controllers control."

Mandy nodded. She felt the knot in her throat. "We tell Aldina after," she added, low, the decision tasting like metal. "Not before. Just in case he's watching..."

Mercedes's eyes flashed hot. "Right. If he thinks we're playing him... he won't hurt us first. He'll go for my mom. And yours." She said it like a weather report and swallowed it like it wasn't.

They rode the moped with their helmets down and their plans compacted to a single tight idea: meet, absorb, survive, inform. The city's noise didn't sit right; the traffic seemed to operate on a half-second delay, horns coming after the near-misses; the crosswalk ticks went fast-slow-fast like a metronome handled by a drunk. A tram's pantograph sparked blue across the overhead wire—one crisp snap—and then the line hummed back into its usual complaint.

He chose a place that said **Don't** in five different textures: a wedge of land where the canal met a forgotten service yard, a clump of birch trees with peeling white skin, the skeleton of a half-taken-down billboard leaning over a chain-link fence as if it had just realized how pointless it had been. The city was close enough to see, far enough to ignore them.

Bilal was there, jacket zipped to his throat, hands in the pockets, not moving much. A small paper bag sat on a low concrete block beside him, the kind used for anchoring things that didn't deserve a proper pedestal. No car in sight; no obvious spotter. Which meant the spotter had chosen *good* places to hide.

"You're early," he said.

"You said now," Mercedes shot back. "This is now."

He took a small folded square of paper from his pocket and pinched it between two fingers like it might bite. When he held it out, Mandy didn't take it. Mercedes did, quick, because it felt safer to be fast than to wonder.

On the paper: a string of numbers, then another, and beneath them a shorthand map sketch only someone who'd walked the lanes would recognize—alley mouth, dumpsters, the way the streetlight failed on the third post down.

"Burn it when you're done," he said.

Mandy's pulse climbed the stairs inside her throat. "Why paper?"

"Because paper doesn't ping," he said. "And because if you drop it into the canal it doesn't try to text your friends goodbye."

"Why earlier?" Mercedes asked. "Why now?"

He shrugged, which wasn't a real answer. "Sometimes the air changes," he said. "When it does, people with calendars start to sweat."

"Are you human enough to sweat?" Mercedes said, and it was half a taunt and half a test to see if he would let her draw blood.

"Sometimes," he said. "When it matters."

The cranes groaned in a little breeze that didn't feel like it belonged to weather. Mandy felt the pressure behind her eyes change the way it did when you went up too fast in an elevator. She blinked to clear it, and the blink didn't give the world back in the right order. The gray around things thickened. The edges of the van fuzzed as if they had been cut out of a different picture and pasted badly into this one.

She opened her mouth to say *It's happening* and her lips were heavy, like saying things cost a tax her voice couldn't afford.

"Mandy?" Mercedes asked, but the word sounded long and faraway and underwater.

The lights on the cranes stuttered once, a micro-strobe. In the stutter—too short to be light, too long to be a blink—her father arrived.

Not from a direction. Not with footsteps. He was just... at the edge of the road, one hand lifted as if he'd been about to knock on a door that wasn't there. The same jacket. The tired kindness in the mouth. The grief in the eyes that was never for himself.

He pointed.

Not at the paper. Not at Bilal. At Mandy's phone where it lay face down in her pocket like a sleeping animal. Her screen woke without being told, and the map slid into being as if a hand much larger than hers had swiped it open. Three points pulsed red in the thin city diagram, the triangle she knew by now even when it was gone—stairwell, café window, doorframe with glittered glass. The lines hummed toward a center, and for the first time Mandy felt the map tug not just her attention but her balance. *There,* the tug said. *There, there, there.*

Her ears filled with a whine so precise it might as well have been a pure math tone. The hum in the road went silent and then came back in the wrong octave. Her stomach tried to climb her spine. She swallowed hard and her throat miscounted.

Her father's hand trembled—the first time she'd seen the overlay do anything she could call imperfect—and then steadied. He traced the triangle a second time, slower, knuckle making a small arc in air. The points pulsed in answer.

Mandy tried to say *Okay* and instead time dropped her.

The ground didn't move. She did. She felt herself slide, not down but sideways, like she'd stepped between floorboards into a gap wider than logic. The world did a shiver like film at the end of a reel.

Then nothing.

"Mands," Mercedes said, and now her voice finally broke. "Please, please—hey—please."

Mandy's head thumped onto her shoulder. Her eyes rolled slowly up. No witty comment came to rescue anybody.

"I need to—" Mercedes's hands fluttered uselessly over Mandy's face, the way you fan a fire that has decided to die.

Mercedes's vision tunneled to a keyhole around Mandy's face. Blood had slicked under Mandy's nostril and along her upper lip, ornament and wound. Her eyes were closed—not sleep closed, *off* closed. The hum in the yard climbed an octave she did not have a name for. Her hands shook and she wanted to scream at her own hands.

"What happened to her?" Bilal's voice, close. He had moved, he was kneeling now, one palm hovering over Mandy's shoulder like he wanted to touch and didn't dare. "What is this?"

"You tell me," Mercedes spat, clutching Mandy's hoodie at the shoulders, trying to lift, to shake, to wake. She hated herself while she did it. "You and your coordinates and your—your *threats—*"

"She's bleeding," he said, as if Mercedes hadn't noticed. "She was... here and then she wasn't—" He stopped, jaw tight.

"I don't—" Mercedes started. "She does this," Mercedes snapped at him, wild, as if that accusation might make a usable world. "She goes away. But not like this. Not this long."

Bilal didn't move for one heartbeat. Two. His eyes flicked to the blood and then to the tiny smear on the dropped phone's glass. "She needs a doctor," he said, and whatever plan he'd been carrying in his jacket for the next hour disintegrated like sugar in hot tea. "Help me get her up."

Together, they maneuvered Mandy into something like upright. She was too heavy and too light at once. The world had narrowed to the space from the fence to a van hidden across the roads.

He got the van door with one hand and lifted Mandy's legs with the other. He was stronger than he looked, which made Mercedes hate him more. They worked with a clumsy efficiency neither would remember later. Mandy's head lolled, blood a thin cut line now, and Mercedes dabbed at it with the sleeve of her own jacket because she had no tissues and no pride.

"Seat belt," Bilal said, almost gentle. His hands did the buckle she couldn't manage. The van smelled like dust and an old orange peel. He wheeled them out without headlights for ten seconds that felt like a hundred years, then clicked them on and merged into the city as if the city had been waiting for him to arrive to start the next scene.

No one spoke. The van's engine sounded like a swallowed sob. Mercedes held Mandy's hand and told herself she could feel pressure back—a squeeze, a whisper.

At the emergency entrance, light and noise and authority assaulted them. Mercedes hated authority; she craved it now like sugar. "She fainted," she announced to the air, to the triage nurse, to God, to anybody. "Her nose—she's bleeding—she won't wake—"

Forms were shoved toward her like shields. A nurse with lashes too perfect to be a nurse's only trait guided them to a cot, and another took Mandy's vitals with the detached speed of someone who had watched too many kids bleed from too many kinds of holes. A doctor asked questions that assumed pills or parties or parents. Mercedes answered with a blend of truth and omission that didn't add up, and the doctor frowned because doctors don't like math that won't resolve.

"Family?" a second nurse asked.

"I'm her sister," Mercedes lied with a straight face. It fit. It always had.

"What about you?" the nurse asked Bilal.

"Nothing," he said. "Nobody."

The nurse blinked at the grammar of that, then moved on because the emergency room was a mechanism that didn't need backstory to run.

They were separated by a curtain and the story of their lives. When the rush settled into the slow drip of waiting, Mercedes sat in the plastic chair by the bed and watched the line on Mandy's monitor decide not to scare her. She wiped the last of the blood from Mandy's lip, then clutched the tissue like she might need proof later that this happened.

After a while, she realized Bilal hadn't left. He stood near the far wall with his hands in his pockets again—pose or self-control, who knew—eyes on the door, then on Mandy, then on the door again.

"Why are you being nice?" she asked, the words scraping her throat on the way out.

"You're hot, then cold. You pick places that smell like dead fish and you hand us calendars and threats and then you help us like—" She bit the rest off because there wasn't a safe thing to put after *like.*

He kept his eyes on the lane markers. "Nice can be free," he said.

"No it isn't," she shot back. "At least not with you. I feel like I'll pay for it later."

He exhaled through his nose. "Then I'm renting."

"It's confusing," she said, fiercer now. "You are confusing. You text like you're both god and the janitor."

"That's because I am neither," he said. "I am the guy whose phone is always on three percent and still won't die."

"Why us," she asked, and it came out as a question about more than the job.

His fingers tightened on the wheel a millimeter. He thought for a long time for someone who was driving with purpose. When he answered, it was a half-answer, and it opened a door and then stood in it.

"Because you look like no one should be afraid of you," he said. "Because you walk like you believe you are a blur. Because the city eats girls who are blurs." He paused. "Because I didn't have a choice."

"Liar," she said, but her voice was tired. "Everyone has a choice."

He shook his head once, and there was a flicker of something in his eyes that made the hair along her arms stand up. He sat in the chair across from her without being invited and leaned forward with his elbows on his knees in the kind of posture men use when they want to look smaller. "When I was thirteen," he said slowly, "I learned how to put my little brother to bed without turning on the lights, because the lights meant the landlord would know we were home. My mom worked nights and days that pretended to be nights. I made noodles a thousand ways. I borrowed money once the wrong way. And then the people with better jackets than me said, *you're good at carrying things.*"

"Cartel," Mercedes said, not a question. "Sable Line."

He didn't agree. He didn't deny. The silence was an admission with a hood on. "They do not love me," he said carefully. "They have a leash with my brother's name on it."

"So you hurt girls," she said, bitterness like metal on her tongue.

"So I pick the ones who look like they will survive," he said, and finally there was heat, ugly heat. "Do you think I choose the ones who will break? Do you think I don't look at your faces and try to... weigh?" He exhaled. "You want a villain, there are doors upstairs with names on them. I am a hallway."

She hated that the sentence made sense. She hated that her heart did the stupid soft thing anyway, the one that wanted to lay its cheek on a story and pretend it could rest there.

"Why are you telling me any of this?" she asked. "Why right now."

"Because the paper is in her pocket and I need you to understand the game is not over because she fainted," he said, colder again, the heat replaced by control. "And because—" He stared at the curtain and chose the smallest truth. "Because I don't want your friend to die." He held her eyes for a beat. "Or you."

The curtain rattled. A nurse with eyebrows in a perpetual question poked her head in. "She's stable," she said, tone brisk enough to file nails on. "Fluids, a mild sedative to interrupt a possible vasovagal thing. Labs look okay. We keep her for observation for a couple of hours. When she wakes up, you can take her home."

Mercedes almost cried out of pure relief. "Thank you," she said, and meant it in a way that felt foreign.

The nurse's eyes flicked to Bilal and paused. "Family only," she said, soft but the kind of soft that didn't move when you pushed it.

He stood. "Understood."

He got to the door and stopped, half-turned. "Do not miss the next text," he said to Mercedes without looking at her. "You won't get two."

"Don't call it a text like it's a friendly thing," she said. "It's a leash."

He considered that, then shrugged, an unknown expression on his face. When he was gone, she let herself fold in half over the arm of the chair and cry into her own elbow in a way that didn't disturb the monitors. She hated him. She hated that she didn't hate him enough.

Mandy's eyelids fluttered. Mercedes straightened so fast her neck popped. "Hey," she whispered, wiping her face with the clean square of her sleeve. "Hey, babe. You took a trip."

Mandy blinked hard, confusion resolving into recognition the way pixels become an image. "Where...?"

"Hospital," Mercedes said. "You did your vanishing trick but more intense. Blood and... out. You scared me."

Mandy closed her eyes again, just long enough to gather herself, then opened them with a steadier hinge. "Did he—"

"He brought us," Mercedes said. "Don't make me say it twice."

Mandy nodded, small and slow. "Paper still on me?"

Mercedes patted her hoodie pocket, gentle. "Yeah. With the numbers."

"Good," Mandy whispered. She swallowed. "We tell Aldina. Right away."

"Yeah," Mercedes said. "We will."

Mandy turned her head slightly, grimacing at a monitor wire that pulled. "Did he say anything? While I was out?"

Mercedes stared at the curtain where he'd stood, the shadow he'd left like a thumbprint on the air. "He said he didn't want you to die," she said finally. "And that we shouldn't miss the next... leash."

Mandy let out a breath that might have been laughter and might have been pain. "So we bring scissors," she murmured, and Mercedes surprised herself by smiling.

"Scissors," she said. "Batman's waiting."

Mandy shut her eyes for a beat and in the darkness saw the triangle again, and the way the center had juddered, like a heart that skipped a beat and then pretended it hadn't. The countdown's red ghosts drifted behind her lids, not numbers now, not exactly—more like pins on a map trying to teach her a language she hadn't learned yet.

"Mercedes," she said, very softly.

"Yeah?"

"When it takes me," Mandy said, "if it keeps taking me longer—"

"It won't," Mercedes said, because she had decided it. "I won't let it."

Mandy nodded like the promise was physics that would hold. She drifted then—thin sleep, the kind that let sounds in—and in that shallow water she felt, not saw, her father's hands again, the two index fingers touching, that impossible gesture, as if to say: Hold the line.

CHAPTER 14

Mercedes signed the discharge form with a hand that still trembled and steered Mandy through the automatic doors like she was carrying glass without hands. Outside, the night felt scrubbed, too bright around the edges, like the hospital lights had followed them to the curb. They did not talk on the short ride, only breathed in uneven counterpoint. When they reached Mandy's building, they both took in a deep breath.

"You don't have to," Mandy began.

Mercedes snorted. "I'm not leaving you on a cliffhanger," she said, and the smile she gave was a little crooked and a little brave. "Come on."

They climbed the stairs instead of taking the elevator. Stairs felt honest. At the door, Mercedes hesitated, brushed hair out of her eyes, and knocked with her knuckles because keys felt too loud. Mandy's mother opened on the second knock, worry already assembled on her face for them being out for too long, then rearranged into something like relief and something like we will talk later. She kissed Mandy's hair, hugged Mercedes with one arm in that way she had that made you feel included without being adopted, and went to make tea because of the cold outside, oblivious of the one seeping into their bones.

Olle heard voices and appeared in the hallway, socks sliding, notebook clutched to his chest. He stopped when he saw Mercedes. The stop was full-body. Eyes widened, shoulders squared, mouth remembered how to smile two beats too late.

"Hey," Mercedes said, soft in a way she did not give away to many people.

"Okay," Olle said, which was not an answer but the only answer he could manage. His ears went pink. He looked at Mandy and recalibrated into big-brother mode. "You look... pale." He frowned at himself. "Empirically paler than your baseline."

"Hospital fluorescent chic," Mandy said. "I need you."

He nodded once, serious now. "Kitchen table. Maps."

They gathered in their usual war room, the table by the window with its flaking white paint and the view of a courtyard tree that tried new leaves every year like it had hope no one had told it it should not. Olle had cleared a space with unusual neatness. A city map lay open, thumbtacked at four corners. Over it, he had taped a printed lattice of the power grid, grey lines crossing like veins, plus a second transparent sheet he had drawn on in pen, triangles etched and labeled. A calculator watched from the placemat like a small rectangular judge. The delta tau ledger he had been keeping for Mandy, columns of dates and lost seconds, was open at the top of the page, today's line still blank.

Mercedes hovered and tried to look at the map instead of at Olle. She knew of the secret crush he harbored inside of him, how when she looked at him, it made him hop internally, and she did not want him to hop out of his brain right now. Not when they needed all their wits to understand this. She folded her arms to trap her hands. Mandy sat, pulled her hoodie tighter, and slid the folded square of paper, the coordinates, from her pocket to the table like it might burn through the wood.

Olle did not touch the paper. He looked at Mandy first. "What happened," he said. Not the resigned *what now*. The scientist's *give me the data.*

She told him. The yard's stutter. Her father by the corrugated wall. The countdown's leap, the way the map had snapped into her head like a sticker peel, the center that jittered sideways, the twin fingers pressed together, the cold, the way the world had cut out and then cut back in wrong. She told him about the hospital and the monitor and the nurse with weaponized eyebrows. She told him about the paper with numbers and the way Bilal carried her like a parcel he was ashamed of.

Olle wrote while she spoke, fast without being messy, his pencil a metronome. He did not ask her to slow down. He never asked her to relive what hurt longer than she had to. When she finished, he slid his ledger toward her and tapped yesterday's total. "You lost one minute, fifty-three seconds during the shed episode," he said quietly. "At the yard," he hesitated, did the mental math she could practically see moving across his eyes, and wrote: **$\Delta\tau = 2{:}07$**. "Two minutes seven seconds. That puts you over five lost minutes in a forty-eight hour window."

Drop moved.
Tomorrow 17:40.
Wait for instruction.

"Is that... bad?" Mercedes asked, wary, like the answer might bite if she reached for it.

"I do not have enough data to say bad with a probability I like," Olle said. Then, because he was not a machine and he was learning to translate himself for them, "But it makes me nervous."

Mandy touched the ledger, the touch that said I see what you are trying to do for me. "Tell me your current theory," she said. "The real one."

Olle exhaled, a tiny fog. He planted both hands on the table next to the map. "I definitely do not think you are seeing a ghost," he said, and his voice had moved to the tone he used when he presented in class. Careful, precise, almost gentle even when the content was not. "I think Dad is alive in a different branch. Parallel, not past. Another track on the paper," he added, and slid his fingers under the map to lift a corner, then curved the sheet into a subtle arc. "We are not rewinding. We are changing lanes. That is why nothing in our past rearranges itself when you see him. No photos fade. No people blink. Everything is present, and present can fork."

Mercedes stared like he had grown a second head. "So there are two roads. Or a thousand roads," she said slowly, groping for terms she hated but needed. "And her dad is on one shouting across the median."

"Not shouting," Olle said. "Signaling. And signaling is expensive. There is a cost, call it delta tau. When he reaches across, your time here shaves off you. Not backwards into your past, but skipped forward in your perception. Micro blackouts. That is why it feels like jumping a few steps on a staircase and finding your foot already touching a rung you did not remember."

Mandy swallowed. "That is also why I... left tonight."

He nodded. "It is the longest skip so far. It correlates with something else, energy spikes. You told me about the triangle in the shed. I overlaid the possible coordinates, and they matched a few blast sites from the news." He tapped three red circled points he had inked on the transparent sheet. "They form a triad around a lattice node. Every time there is a triad like that, the grid in that area shows a measurable surge, then a brief brownout. Your episodes line up within minutes of those surges. Not perfectly," he added, sincere enough not to lie to make it neater, "but enough to suggest causality."

Mandy leaned over the map, felt the hum of it through her elbows. "So the blasts," she began.

"Open windows," Olle said. "If you make three spikes at mapped lines, you can stabilize a longer window. He can reach. You are the only one who can see, because you are an Anchor." He looked at her, and his eyes were too old for his face for a second. "Anchors happen where the branches disagree about life and death, or simply… loss. In ours, Dad died and you lived. In his, it's possible that you died and he lived. That kind of mismatch could be capable of lowering noise. So the channel finds you, not Mom or me."

Mercedes breathed out hard, like someone had just stepped off her chest. "That is horrible. And kind of beautiful," she said, grimacing at herself.

"It is physics pretending to be poetry," Olle said simply.

Mandy gripped the edge of the table until the wood bit. "If he is reaching to warn me, warn us, then the numbers," she pulled the square of paper free and laid it flat, careful with it like it could be contagious, "and these. What are they?"

Olle unfolded the square. In neat block digits, someone had written **59.3347, 18.0631**. No labels. No name. Just two numbers that looked like nothing and were everything. He typed them into his phone with a thumb that did not tremble. A small red pin dropped on a digital map.

He did not say the place out loud. He turned his phone so they could see. The pin sat on a narrow service lane two blocks off the downtown mall, hemmed by a substation feeder line and a cluster of commercial waste cans. A short substation spur ran like a tether from the main lattice right past it.

"Center," he said softly. He tilted the transparent triangle sheet and slid it until the three plotted blasts from the last week, stairwell, café, cracked doorway, circled the pin like hounds. The centroid sat almost perfectly at the coordinates on the paper. "If you place a device here while the other three nodes are flaring, it would not be a fourth explosion," he said. "It would be a collector. It would pull the energy they are dumping into the grid into one focus. You could stabilize a window big enough for longer overlays. Maybe more."

"More like what?" Mercedes asked, already knowing she did not want the answer.

"Information with less loss," Olle said. He hesitated, then added what the math pointed to whether he liked it or not. "Or, if someone had a coil to hold it, more than information."

Mandy's skin went cold the way it had in the shed when her father drew the line in the air. She pressed her fingers to the coordinates like she could smudge them away. "Why the countdown," she asked, voice thin, "if there are coordinates?"

"Both," Olle said, and this time his voice carried the change in their theory. "The overlay piggybacks on the clock jitter in your phone because clocks are a universal substrate. He uses that to send two kinds of information through the same tiny pipe. The coordinates are what you saw on the map, the triangle and the center. The countdown is not a schedule for bomb times. It is a budget for you. It is an estimate of how much of your subjective time will be shaved off by the next contact. Think of it as a cost meter. When it drops, he is warning you of the toll, not telling you when the city will shake. That is why the digits jump when you feel the pull. They reflect the price you are about to pay."

Mercedes stared at the phone like it had become a small animal with too many teeth. "So the numbers are not when, they are where and how much that information costs me."

"Yes," Olle said. "How much of the here-Mandy we may lose in the moment. Not forever, but enough to matter if it stacks. The where still comes through as pins and shapes. The when of explosions belongs to whoever is placing them and to the grid. The countdown is Dad trying to protect here-Mandy by making the cost visible."

Mandy let out air that had been trapped under her ribs. The fear shifted shape, no smaller, only named. "He is trying to stop this. Not make it happen. Or he is trying to stop us being the ones who make it happen."

time-loss entries (Δt)
TODAY

"Maybe both," Olle said. "If his branch saw a triad like this end badly, he is steering us away from their future by getting us to choose differently now. He cannot change his past or ours. But he can make our present different from the future they got."

"Lane change, not time travel," Mercedes said, almost under her breath. "Man, I wish I had listened to Ms. Von Post's lecture now, maybe then I wouldn't feel like I'd have a heart attack with all this crazy information overload."

Mandy drank tea that had gone lukewarm and did not taste it. "We have to tell Aldina about the center," she said. "We have to not make the drop."

"We have to not get my mom killed as well," Mercedes said, sharp with love and fear. "That was the price he named. He meant it."

"I know," Mandy said. The admission made her shoulders hurt. "But Aldina said she'll protect us, we have to believe it."

Olle slid the ledger down the table and tapped a new line he had started. **Window triads equal danger. Center coordinates equal lever. Countdown equals Mandy's cost.** "I think the center is the lever," he said. "If you do not place the satchel there, the triad cannot lock. The window will open and fail. The cost to you," he added, looking at Mandy's face, "might go up in that moment. He might try harder to break through. You will need to be ready to ride it."

"I can do it," she said. It was not courage so much as the absence of room for anything else.

Mercedes huffed out through her teeth, then leaned back, then forward again like a wave that had not made up its mind. "Okay, this is all… too much for my simple-minded head, but there is one more thing that's like, completely hammering at my brain and I need an answer or else I will implode."

Olle made a gesture as if to go on, and Mandy gave her a knowing look with a sigh, already anticipating the train of thought Mercedes' mind had found itself at. She turned to Olle. "Since you may as well be a certified genius, after that hospital conversation, do you think he cares about me?" she said, daring him to lie.

Olle blinked. "Who?"

"Bilal," she said, and regretted making it sound like a middle school question the second it left her mouth.

Olle swallowed, eyes flicking to her face and away like looking straight at an eclipse. "I think he is dangerous to you and also not indifferent. Those can coexist."

"Great," Mercedes said. "A hallway with feelings."

Mandy's mouth twitched. She made it stop. "Regardless, the point is the plan," she said. "We cannot do the drop. But we cannot simply not show. Even if he somehow has a moral ground and his own sob-story, it doesn't change the fact that he *is desperate.* He *will* choose another courier. The plan will still focus."

"So we stall," Mercedes said. "We pretend to be on the plan, and get him to Aldina somehow. She will get the answers for the rest. Maybe get him to act on our side. Make him understand the consequences."

"Batman time," Mandy said, half a joke and all a decision.

Mandy reached across the table and folded the paper again along its crease, then folded it once more, smaller this time, smaller still, until it was a little white square she could hide in her palm. She felt a steadiness grow under the ache in her head like a platform had been lowered into place.

Olle looked at her, and the pride in his eyes was a quiet thing, like a lamp left on in a hallway to keep the dark honest. "You need to rest every hour until the meet. Hydration. Salt. If it pulls you again, sit on the floor. Reduce fall risk. You need to get all your energy back up."

"Doctor Olle," Mercedes said, unable not to smile at him now. His ears did their pink thing again, which only made her smile harder.

Mandy's phone buzzed on the table.

All three of them stared at it as if it had spoken from a mouth.

Mercedes whispered, "Well, fuck."

Mandy turned it over with a finger.

Unknown:
Drop moved. Tomorrow. 17:40. Wait for instruction.

The words sat there, ordinary and obscene.

No one spoke for a long count. Somewhere in the courtyard a child laughed at something that did not deserve that much joy. The sound felt like a dare.

Mandy pressed the small white square of coordinates into her fist until the corners bit. "Tomorrow," she said, and the word made the room colder. "We have a day."

Olle shut his notebook and turned the map toward himself like a shield. "Then we use it," he said. "We do not panic. We plan."

Mercedes cracked her knuckles, a ritual that always made Mandy want to tell her to stop and that tonight sounded like a blessing. "Scissors," she said, and the grin she gave had teeth. "And a bat signal nobody sees."

CHAPTER 15

They chose a place where sound couldn't decide what to be.

The underpass lay three blocks off the tram line that fed the mall, a concrete throat where traffic roared overhead and the echo below broke words into sharp pieces. Graffiti layered the pillars like a palimpsest of arguments no one had won. Water bled from a crack in the retaining wall and made a thin, persistent thread into a grate. It smelled like cold and rubber and something metallic you could not name.

Aldina liked it because it had angles. Sight lines. Two exits if you counted the scramble up the embankment to the bike path. One way in if you were the kind of person who thought the straightest line was always the fastest. She had walked it twice that afternoon with her hood up and her hair braided back the way she wore it on long crime-scene nights. She paced out distances under her breath and marked her place between pillars with a piece of tape the same color as the concrete. It looked like nothing until you knew what it was.

Mandy and Mercedes liked it because it felt like neutral ground that hated everyone equally.

"You're sure?" Aldina asked when they met in the shadow just out of view of the closest streetlight. Her voice was down in that register she used when she was telling a rookie, quietly, how not to step on evidence. "He comes if you call?"

Mandy rubbed her hands together hard enough to warm bone. "He comes if Mercedes calls," she said. "He thinks she's his trouble."

Mercedes stood with her jaw lifted in a scowl. "He does not," she said. Her face was flushed with the thought, but she chose not to acknowledge it. "What do I say?"

"You say you can't breathe," Mandy said, and hated the accuracy of it. "You say you're alone, and you're near the mall, and you can't carry this by yourself. You don't define 'this.' He'll fill it in with what scares him."

Aldina nodded.

"What if he doesn't come alone?" Mercedes asked. "What if he brings a… friend?"

Aldina's hand settled on the small of her back where the gun lay in its holster, more a touchstone than a weapon. "Then I will make it a very short conversation," she said. "He won't pull on you here, I know how to defend well."

Mercedes took out her phone and stared at the screen until her nerve and her need found the same frequency. She typed with both thumbs, fast.

Mercedes:
It's too much. I'm near the mall. I can't. Please.

She watched the typing bubble appear, blink, vanish, return. When the reply came, it had no punctuation and no comfort, only direction.

Bilal:
Where

Her pulse went heavier. She typed the cross street by the underpass and added a lie: **Alone**.

"Put it away," Aldina said, already moving. "You two go ahead down. Fifty meters. Pillar four. Stand where the light breaks. He'll be able to see your faces and not who's behind the column."

"You've done this before," Mercedes said, irreverent with fear.

"Of course," Aldina said. She did not say the times she had wished she had done it a minute sooner.

Mandy touched Mercedes's wrist, a signal they'd used since they were twelve: together, or not at all. They walked down the ramp, shoes loud, like they wanted whoever was waiting to know they weren't sneaking. The underpass took their outlines and turned them into rumors. They stopped between pillars three and four where the streetlight broke into a pale trapezoid on the ground.

"Now the hysterics," Mercedes muttered.

"You don't have to—" Mandy began.

Mercedes rolled her eyes and swatted the air. "I'm good at theater." She took a breath, then let it out as a shudder. She pressed the back of her hand to her mouth and made a sound that was not crying but that had crying in it. She bent a little at the waist. She turned and looked back the way they'd come as if afraid of the wrong thing. It was convincing enough to make Mandy's body want to catch her even though she was not falling.

A dark figure peeled off the shadow near the ramp like a splice in film. He moved fast down the grade, light catching on his cheekbone, on the zipper of his jacket, on the line of his throat when he looked from one girl to the other and calculated the distance to both. He looked like a problem you would take personally. He looked like he had stopped sleeping a long time ago.

"Mercedes," he said, and there was something in it that was not ownership and was not tenderness and was still a word he would not have spent on anyone else.

She shoved her phone at him like it had burned her. "I can't," she said. "You said tomorrow and now it's today and you said you'd keep my mom alive and I can't—" She pushed the words out until they broke against the wall of his chest. "I thought you liked me," she added, and it came out high, an insult and a plea. "I thought you—" She cut it off with a sound that could have been a laugh if it wanted to be mean. "Forget it."

Bilal reached like he would steady her and then remembered who he was supposed to be and put his hands into his pockets as if to cuff them there. "No one else gets this done," he said, the flatness back. "That's the job."

"What job," Aldina said, stepping out from behind the pillar with the quiet of someone who knew the way a room breathed. The word did a strange thing to the air. It made it choose sides.

She stood with her feet set like a fighter and her hands visible and her badge hidden and her eyes on him in a way that made most men take one involuntary step back. Bilal did not. His mouth tightened in a way that said he counted exits every time he entered anything, and he found both of hers immediately.

"Who the hell—" he began.

"Bilal Hernandez," she said. "Turn around. Keep your hands in view."

His body stilled the way prey animals still. He did not jerk. He did not run. He slowly turned to the direction of the voice and took in the gun, the woman, the narrow path she had stepped from, the two girls behind him. He lifted his hands to shoulder height. The move was graceful and clean, like he had practiced compliance in a mirror.

"You do not want to do this here," he said. It did not sound like a threat. It sounded like advice.

"I do not want to do this at all," Aldina said, and in her voice lived three years of funerals that never happened because there were no bodies left to stand around. "But I am going to."

Mandy's mouth went dry. This was the first time she had seen Aldina point a gun at a person who had a name in her mouth. The weapon in her hands did not look like the ones in shows. It looked present. It looked applied.

Mercedes moved without thinking. She stepped so she was not next to Bilal, not in front of him, but a little off his shoulder, inside his reach, as if her body could be a vote.

"Stop there," Aldina said, and Mercedes stopped.

"This is a mistake," Mandy said, and she heard the tin in her own voice and hated it.

Aldina did not look at Mandy. She did not look at Mercedes. Her eyes were on Bilal's face. Something in her expression changed. A shadow moved across it and then stayed. Mandy only recognized it because she had seen her own mother's face when old photographs pulled air out of a room.

"Do you know a bus route called 54," Aldina asked. The question cut diagonally across the moment so sharply that Mandy blinked. "Do you. Answer me."

"I know a lot of routes," Bilal said, and Mandy understood with a jolt that he was doing the same thing with his voice that Aldina was doing with her eyes. He was trying to keep control through familiarity.

"My father drove a bus," Aldina said. "He died doing it. He died two stops from home. An explosion under the second bench tore him in half. He was wearing a yellow vest because he had been fixing the ticket machine when they were between shelters. There were six passengers. There was not enough left of any of them to fill a single body bag. The case was dropped. Transferable DNA, they said. The cameras were out. But there were names in the margins. Your name has been underlined in my house so long the paper is thin."

Bilal's mouth tightened. "I did not place that device."

"You carried others," she said. "You will carry one today. You think you have no choice. I am here to tell you there is a choice and you are looking at it."

The gun did not waver. She had moved three steps closer without seeming to move. Mandy could see the tendons in Aldina's forearms, the way her breath sat under her ribs.

"Code 6004," Aldina said, and the words were not for anyone else. She had said them to herself in the mirror and to the wall of her room full of pinned photographs and lines of red string. She had said them to the air. Saying them here made them real. Death without suspicion of crime. If she did it right, the report would read like an accident.

"Stop," Mandy said. "Stop. Listen. He is not the top. He is the cord someone else is holding."

Aldina did not blink.

Mercedes took one step forward and her voice cracked open. "They have his brother," she said, the sentence coming out on a sob she did not try to fix. "He said it to me. I did not believe him, but I do now. Sable Line has his little brother. If he fails, they do not just hurt him. They hurt a child. You kill him here and it does not end anything. It just ends him."

The look on Aldina's face shifted again. New information spoke to the part of her that cataloged evidence even in rage. The gun stayed up. Mandy could see the micro tremor in the barrel now. It was not fear. It was effort.

"You are still going to carry a satchel into a crowd," Aldina said, voice flat. "You will still take a step and then another because someone texted you to."

Bilal looked at the ground between his shoes for a long second. When he lifted his head, the hardness he wore like a jacket was still there, but it no longer hid everything. There was a tiredness under it that did not ask to be seen.

She kept the gun holstered and let him see that decision sit between them. "You are the leash, not the hand. And the hand is using you to lay bodies down in geometries that don't look random to anyone who can add. You're going to tell me where the hand will be standing at six tonight."

"That's not how this works," he said. "You don't get to—"

"Code 6004," Aldina said, quiet, like a confession to herself. The digits hovered in the cold air like breath. "Do you know what that means? 'Death without suspicion of crime.' It's what they write when they can't prove what they know. When the system puts on earmuffs and hums until the case goes quiet."

His eyes flicked once to the holster, back to her mouth. "So what," he said, and the two words landed with less certainty than he meant. "You shoot me here? You think that solves your math?"

"No," she said. "I think following you like a shadow until I can grab the sleeve of the person who thinks they can use kids and women as clean hands solves it." The rhythm of her speech altered, a hitch. Memory slid its fingers into her throat. "And I think when I look at you in this light, I see a woman pushing a pram across a crosswalk when the light was green, and a bus driver who didn't drink and didn't speed and died on a Tuesday because someone's little metal kingdom needed to be bigger by one street."

The underpass shifted focus. The drip at the grate got louder. The traffic above went vague, like it had been moved a lane over. Aldina's gaze locked to Bilal's face and something in it cracked the way windshields crack in slow motion in videos you wish you had not clicked on. Her fingers ghosted toward the holster, then gripped air an inch short like she had caught herself on a railing at the top of a stair.

Mercedes stepped forward without thinking. She lunged and planted herself in the line between the two of them. She raised both hands like a referee at a school match and shook her head so hard her earrings rattled. "Please, Bilal," she blurted, voice breaking in three places. "Help her stop this, so we can all just... we can all just *breathe* for once. Your brother needs you without this life over your head."

Bilal looked at Mercedes, something in his eyes softening. He took a moment to think, and after a moment of hesitation, forced his eyes back on Aldina. "There are spotters in the mall," he said. "Two. If something goes off-script, they complete a triad. It's not just one thing exploding. It's three. That's how they get what they need." The words seemed to hurt him just to say.

Aldina's jaw worked. You could see the old training—triage, prioritization, pressure—argue with the hot animal that wanted tit for tat. You could see how practice wins, or loses, by a centimeter. She shut her eyes. The underpass breathed once. She opened them. She holstered the gun with a motion that looked like it cost her more than pulling it.

"You're going to walk with me," she said to Bilal. "You're going to put me near their line and not inside it. You're going to identify the two spotters, and you're going to keep your hands where they can't get you killed. If you run, I assume you're running for them. If you lie, I will know."

"They'll see me with you," he said. "They'll—"

"You'll peel off before we go above ground," she said. "You'll tip me and then go where you're supposed to go, and we'll intercept there." She looked at the girls. "You are not going into the mall until I say. If he's right and there are spotters, they'll want you as an excuse to lock the triangle."

"Like a key," Mandy said, and the word felt correct in a way that made her stomach jerk.

"Like bait," Aldina said.

"We're not good bait," Mercedes protested in automatic pride.

"You're the best," Aldina said, and made it a compliment and a warning at once. "You don't look like trouble until you're already in the room."

Bilal's mouth twisted in a private thought. He glanced at Mercedes as if he wanted to apologize that he'd been part of teaching her that lesson the worst way and did not know how to ask permission to try.

"Who is the hand," Aldina asked, quieter. "Your boss's boss."

He shook his head. "You think they tell me names? I'm a courier. I pick up, I don't ask."

"You don't need a name," Mandy said, quiet, because she had seen the triangle and the way the lines pulled. "You need a location."

He looked at her then, really looked, and something sorrow-shaped crossed his features. "You're smarter than I want you to be," he said. "For what's coming."

Aldina cut his line of sight. "Coordinates," she said.

He hesitated, the kind that was not performance. "I don't carry paper twice," he said. "We got burned on a phone last winter. They moved to handwritten only, then eat it." He patted his stomach with dark humor. "Literally."

"You can write it once more," Aldina said, slipping a thin notepad and a short pencil from her coat pocket and holding them out. "Then you can eat it again for all I care."

He took the pencil. His hand did not shake. He wrote quickly without looking around like he trusted his body to remember the street grid as well as his brain. He ripped the page free and handed it not to Aldina, not to Mandy, but to Mercedes, like the act of putting it in her hand made something about the mess his own.

"Two spotters," he said, business now, as if he could get through this with clean nouns. "One at the north escalators by the store with the copper pans in the window. One outside the bathroom corridor by the ATMs. If you see either move at the same time, it's because someone told them the script changed."

"And if the script changes," Aldina said.

"You either leave or you bleed," he said. "There's not a third option."

"Watch me invent one," she said.

He huffed something like a laugh and pinched the bridge of his nose hard enough to whiten his knuckles. Something near-gentle slid into his posture when he lowered his hand and looked at Mercedes again. "You shouldn't have called," he said, and there was a thread of fondness in it you could play a tune on if you wanted.

"Make up your damn mind," she said, but her eyes were wet and furious. "You can't play both sides forever."

"I know," he said. The knowing lived in his shoulders.

Aldina checked the time on the cheap analog watch she wore when she wanted to remember how to count seconds without a screen. "We're done here," she said, decision snapping the air back into shape. "Mercedes, you and Mandy peel off south and cut across two blocks. Do not take the tram. Stay in moving crowds and walk like you have someplace to be. If no one pings you by five-thirty, you go to our secondary meet." She told them the cross street, the coffee cart that stayed open too late, the bench with the leg that wobbled. "If I don't show, you go home. You don't play hero without me."

Mercedes bristled with a readiness that made her look older and younger at once. "Copy," she said, making fun of herself and also not.

"And you," Aldina said to Bilal, hand back near the small of her back, the habit that had kept her alive this long. "We go east along the service road. You peel at the light by the tram barn. If you're not there when I turn my head, I assume you were never born and that makes my night easier."

"Charming," he said, but the line did not land. He looked at Mercedes like he wanted to say something that would make everything that had happened to both of them flatter and simpler. He settled for, "She's right, don't be a hero," which in his mouth almost became a kind of prayer.

"Don't be a coward," she returned, and the corners of his mouth did that almost-smile thing that did not reach his eyes and still made a small change across his whole face.

They broke like a cell dividing. The girls moved south, footsteps purposeful, heads low, the trick of people who wanted to look like they belonged to someplace and not to a plot. Bilal and Aldina walked east together a few strides apart, the proximity that said partnership to anyone dumb and war to anyone paying attention. When they reached the lip of the ramp, he paused and glanced back under the bridge where the girls had been.

"You're not wrong," he said, half to himself. "About the hand. The crime is too calculated for it to be coincidence."

"Good," Aldina said. "I'm bored when I'm right too early."

He peeled off at the light like they'd rehearsed. She watched him until he disappeared into his own shadows, then cut across the bike lane and climbed the steps two at a time to ground level. She felt the old ache in her right knee where she had slipped on a wet tile after a twelve-hour day and laughed at herself in the empty stairwell because she had thought thirty would be later than it turned out to be.

Under the overpass, the drip continued. Above, traffic insisted on its own importance. Between the two, in the narrow space where decisions were made, three people who had no business trusting one another decided to do it anyway for long enough to stop a clock they did not understand.

Aldina walked into the hum of the city on a day that wanted to become evening. The sky had that color you can't name without trying on six wrong words first. On the glass of the mall's entrance, her reflection looked like a person who had already decided how this would go and would be very angry if the universe disagreed.

Behind her, somewhere, Mandy's phone vibrated once like a small animal stretching.

Unknown:
Be ready. Instructions soon.

Mandy didn't answer. She looked at Mercedes. Mercedes rolled her shoulders like a boxer and blew hair out of her eyes. "Showtime," she said.

CHAPTER 16

The service door opened with a tired gasp and exhaled cold air that smelled like detergent and rubber wheels. A narrow corridor ran behind the glossy storefronts, all concrete and fluorescent hum, with a painted line for carts to follow and a taped sheet that said Deliveries in crooked type. Mandy and Mercedes stepped into it like they belonged there, heads up, pace even. Behind them, the mall swallowed its own noise.

Mandy's phone vibrated once.

Unknown:
Left at first fork. Wait by family restroom. Do not enter.

She did not show the text. She just took the left at the scuffed fork and kept moving until the sign for a family restroom appeared over a gray door with a push plate and a stroller symbol. She and Mercedes stopped and stared at the beige paint as if doors could stare back.

Aldina ghosted into view from the far end, a different person than the one who had stood under the bridge with a gun. Her hands were empty. Her eyes were steady. She had shed the heat of that moment and put on the part of her that worked scenes. She did not break stride.

"Two minutes," she said under her breath. "Then I am going to need your bag."

Mercedes nodded once. Mandy nodded too, less because of the instruction and more to make something in her body feel controlled. Her hands were damp. Her mouth tasted like pennies.

The family restroom door clicked, then opened from the inside. Olle stood there in a hoodie that was a size too big and a backpack that pulled his shoulders forward. He had slipped in through a staff entrance Aldina had unlatched with a borrowed badge. He held a plastic grocery sack, knotted tight at the top, and he was trying not to look like a boy who had sneaked into a place he should not be.

Mandy's chest squeezed. "No," she said quietly to Aldina, before she could stop herself. "No. He should not be here."

Aldina contained the flinch. "He is already here," she said. "I called him for a reason. I need his head and my hands. Five minutes. In and out."

"You put him in danger," Mandy said. There was no way to keep the accusation out of her voice. It came wrapped in fear. "If anything happens, if anyone follows us in, he does not even know how to run the right way."

Olle blinked, taking that in and filing it. He did not look offended. He looked like a person making space in his mind for a new variable.

Aldina kept her voice level. "I am not guessing with you in a hallway. I am not cutting a wire in the open. We do this inside, with the lock turned. I have done this before. I am not careless with children."

"He is not a child," Mercedes said softly, surprising them both. "But he is our friend."

Olle flushed. The flush looked like heat and pride and embarrassment in equal measure. "I will be quick," he said to Mandy. "And I will listen. That is my deal. If you say stop, I stop."

The door shut behind them like a held breath. The family restroom was the size of a small bedroom, tiled and echoing, with a changing shelf that folded down from the wall and one high window frosted to milk. The fan made a thin, constant sound. Aldina turned the lock, then set her black canvas go-bag on the folded shelf and unzipped it. Inside were tools as ordinary as they were dangerous in the right sequence: nitrile gloves, evidence pouches, a roll of matte tape, a slim flashlight, a small wrench, a packet of silica, a weighted training pouch used for demonstrations, sealed in clear plastic like a medical supply. She worked with a practiced economy.

"Phones," she said. "Airplane mode. On the counter. Face down. If one of you needs to call out, I will say when."

They did it without protest. Mandy added one thing, because she could not help herself. "If you are about to do something loud, tell me first." Her head still felt tender where the last overlay had rung through her.

"I am not going to be loud," Aldina said. She nodded to the satchel. "Put it up."

Mandy slipped the strap over her head and lifted the gray bag onto the changing shelf beside the go-bag. The weight settled with a dull thud, heavy in a way that made her arms ache. Aldina's eyes flicked to the seams, to the hardware, to the stitching at the corners. She slid on gloves and traced a path along the flap without touching any fastener, thinking three steps ahead the way she did at work.

"No logos," she said. "Custom stitching. Not a courier bag. It looks like one but it is not. Watch me. No surprises."

She eased the flap open on the side with the least strain. No alarms sounded. No pins popped. Inside, a dense foam insert cradled three objects like organs prepared for transplant. Olle leaned in, then checked himself and stood still, hands clasped in front of him so he would not grab anything. Mercedes pressed her knuckles against her lip and stared.

At the center sat a compact core wrapped in layered material that looked like waxed paper and foil. It did not advertise itself and that was the scariest thing about it. To its right lay a ringed assembly the size of a salad plate, copper coils nested inside one another and fixed around a ceramic hub, with two braided leads coiled flat and taped. To the left, a clock module no bigger than a paperback pulsed a quiet green. No beeps. No show.

Aldina breathed out once through her nose. "Core, clock, and something I do not like," she said. She nodded at the ringed device. "That is not a part I have pulled before."

Mandy and Mercedes did not look at each other, but their bodies went tight at the same time. They knew that ring meant something else, from a different set of rules.

Olle tilted his head, eyes narrowing, mind racing but face still. He spoke low. "The clock is clean. No cellular antenna. Probably a simple local loop. The core is insulated. Static could be a problem."

Aldina's glance at him was quick and approving. "Good. You will not create any. Backpacks off the floor. Shoes still. No wool."

She lifted the weighted training pouch from her go-bag. It had been duct taped into a rough rectangle to mimic mass and hold shape. She set it near her elbow like a stand-in waiting for its cue. Then she took out a thin blade and a roll of matte tape and moved with the calm of repetition.

"Sequence," she said to make them focus. "I lift and set. We do not jostle. We do not peel. We do not admire. If I tell you to leave, you leave."

Mandy swallowed and nodded. Her throat felt raw.

Aldina used the blade to nick the foam along the seam where it gripped the core. She worried the slit open with a gloved fingertip, just enough to ease the pressure. The core sat heavy and sloppy under the pretty packaging. It looked like nothing. It could be everything. She set her palms along the sides, applied no more force than a person uses to lift a sleeping cat, and lifted the core a centimeter. It resisted, then yielded, and she slid the weighted pouch into the negative space in one smooth motion. The substitute took the load like it had been made for it. The real core came free into her hands and she did not move her elbows until it hovered over the open evidence tub she had prepared.

"Breathe," she said, and nobody did until the core settled into the tub and the lid kissed closed.

The room did not explode. The fan kept its thin tune. Mandy realized she had been counting heartbeats and could not remember which number she had reached.

Aldina shifted to the ringed device. "This one troubles me," she said. "It is not necessary to detonate. It might be a stabilizer or a sensor. I want it out."

Mandy kept her voice even. "If it is extra, maybe they will not miss it."

"Or maybe it will make them angry," Mercedes said, and then grimaced at herself for saying it out loud.

GUS
PAAES

"I am not in the business of impressing them," Aldina said. "I am in the business of keeping people breathing."

She lifted the coil. Up close it felt heavier than its size suggested, the way dense metals trick your hands. There was a faint ozone tang in the air as it left the foam cradle, a smell that belonged in a lab or a machine room. She set it on a folded towel and taped the leads against the ring so nothing could snag. Then she removed the clock and looked under it to be sure there were no secondaries hidden in the foam. There were not. She reseated the clock, smoothed the foam around it, and closed the flap.

"Weight check," she said. She slid the strap into Mandy's hand. Mandy lifted, tested. The satchel sagged into her like before. A person who knew the exact mass might notice a difference. A person who did not would feel the same ache.

"It passes," Mandy said.

"Good," Aldina said. She wiped the edge of the blade with an alcohol swab, dropped it in a pouch, and locked the evidence tub into her go-bag with the coil nestled beside it, both out of sight. She stripped her gloves and dropped them into a small trash sack she had brought, then knotted it tight and tucked it into the go-bag as well. "We are done."

Mandy took a step toward Olle and kept her voice low. "If anyone comes in, you leave first."

Olle nodded. He was pale but steady. His eyes were bright in that way that meant his head was making a map. "When you feel anything," he said, "when the lights do that thing, you sit. I am serious. You give me thirty seconds to catch up to you."

A knock sounded on the family restroom door. Three short, one long. The pattern they had decided on in the corridor so no one would jump at a cleaner. Aldina cracked the lock and opened the door an inch. A plainclothes officer stood in the gap, eyes scanning the hall, the posture of someone trying to look like he belonged near a restroom. He kept his voice quiet.

"Movement near the skylight run," he said. "Guy in a worker jacket doing loops. Trash can by the stairs has a fresh hinge pin."

Aldina's jaw set. "Thank you. Hold your position. Do not engage unless you have to. I am two minutes out."

He nodded and melted back into the corridor. The door closed again. The fan sounded louder for a second, then normal.

Aldina turned to the girls. "You go back out the way you came. No running. If anyone brushes you, you let them. Crowds are unpredictable when they feel an edge. You do not make sudden movements near bins, benches, or escalators. You put the satchel where the instruction says and you walk."

Mandy swallowed bile. "We are walking into a plan they want to control."

"You are walking like you have always walked," Aldina said. "And you are not alone."

Olle pulled the plastic grocery sack from his backpack and handed it to Mandy. Inside were three identical hoodie strings of dark cotton, each with a small knot at the end. It would look like nothing to anyone else. It meant something to him.

"Tie one around your wrist," he said. "You too, Mercedes. If it drops from your wrist without you moving, I will know you lost time."

The gesture was so Olle it nearly broke her. Mandy tied the string. Mercedes tied hers, eyes stinging and stubborn. Olle held the third string like a reliquary.

Aldina cracked the door and scanned. Clear. She stepped out first, go-bag on her shoulder, posture patient. Mandy followed, the satchel's strap pressing the tender place on her collarbone. Mercedes came last, hand brushing Mandy's elbow as if to steady both of them.

They re-entered the mall's back-run pulse and turned toward the loading bay corridor. The family restroom door clicked behind them and stayed closed. Olle remained inside with his backpack and his notes and his breath held to a count of five. He listened to their footsteps fade and tried not to calculate what thirty seconds might mean.

Back on the public side, the mall felt tighter. People moved with purpose without knowing why. The music under the noise seemed louder and at the same time farther away, like it came from another floor. Mandy scanned without turning her head. The recycling bin near the food court still had its three labeled mouths. A man in a red jacket was not there anymore. A different man leaned near the escalators, texting, then pocketing his phone, then texting again with the same blank face. A woman in a trench coat stood with a stroller, not looking at the watch she kept glancing at.

Mandy's phone pulsed once.

Unknown:
Loading bay corridor. Second door on right. Leave it inside. No pause.

She adjusted the strap, smoothed her face, and headed for the plain door with a battered kick plate and no name. The second door on the right waited like something in a dream that would be obvious once you touched it. A staffer with a cart pushed past and did not see them. Mercedes brushed her sleeve and said sorry and the staffer nodded without looking.

Mandy turned the handle, opened the door, and stepped into a short spur with a single fluorescent tube that stuttered once, then lit. A push bar door marked Emergency Exit Only faced them at the end. The second door on the right stood ajar. She slid in, placed the satchel on the floor just inside, and straightened. Her hand wanted to linger on the strap. She took it away. She and Mercedes stepped back into the main corridor and let the door shut quietly.

They were two girls who had gone to the wrong door and corrected themselves. They walked. Their feet made the right sounds. Their bodies carried the right amounts of air.

At the food court entrance a man with a cap nudged a bin lid half open with two fingers, looked inside, and pushed it closed. At the bottom of the escalator, a boy laid his backpack down, knelt to tie his shoe, and reached under the iron lip of the step with his other hand, then stood and walked away without the backpack. These were small movements anyone could miss. They were the kind of movements Olle saw even when he tried not to.

In the family restroom, he checked his phone despite the airplane icon. He could not help it. He squared his notes on his knee and kept the third string in his lap. He listened to a noise that might have been his own blood.

On the concourse, the crowd thickened in the way late afternoons do when people meet other people in places with chairs. The shimmer at the edge of Mandy's vision rose like heat over asphalt, then faded. The light over her flickered, then steadied. The string on her wrist did not budge. She let breath out and tasted copper again anyway.

Aldina reached the bookshop corridor and saw the man in the worker jacket move with too little aim. He stopped and examined the same fixture twice. He put his hands in his pockets, then took them out. She felt it in her bones before she had the data. He was about to set his small. She spoke into her collar without changing her expression.

"Unit two, eyes on escalators. Unit one, hold food court bin. Do not panic anyone with your face."

She slid her hand into her coat pocket and palmed the small pen clip she had bent earlier, the way a person might hold a worry stone. If she reached a can and found a striker, she would jam it and hope her fingers were faster than his.

The man in the cap at the food court bin lifted the lid again. He had something in his sleeve. It was the motion of someone dropping chewing gum. Aldina moved. Her shoes did not squeak because she never let them.

Closer to the skylight, the boy who had left the backpack under the escalator reached the second floor and looked down. He held his phone like a mirror and did not take a picture. His lips moved like he was counting to himself. The escalator hummed, carrying a group of teenagers with shopping bags and a woman with a baby in a sling and a courier with a box gripped against his hip.

Mercedes's fingers pressed once into Mandy's arm. The pressure said we keep walking and it also said I am afraid. Mandy did not say it back because it was already true.

A group of laughing girls bumped a waste bin and said oops and kept going. The lid jostled. The man in the cap put his hand down and steadied it with the care of someone who thinks he is helping. He touched the hinge a second longer than necessary. Another person who was not looking would have missed it. Aldina did not miss it.

The air felt tighter. The mall's climate control clicked and a different tone layered under the first one, like an instrument tuning.

Olle's string lay still on his lap. He stared at it until the fibers blurred. He pictured triangles linking to a center and he pictured a ringed device removed from a foam cradle and he pictured a clock that did not talk to any cell tower. He did not know how to reconcile those pictures into one story yet. He wanted time to think and hated the word because of what it had started to mean.

At the bottom of the escalator, a small clunk sounded, too soft for the floor and too loud for a pocket. The boy on the second floor walked away and put his phone in his hoodie. The man in the cap moved toward the food court queue as if hungry.

Aldina reached the first bin and lifted the lid with two fingers the way a person lifts a book cover that is not theirs. Inside, nested in the ribbed plastic, a neat metal cup sat where no cup should sit. It was the size of a fist. A spring-loaded striker waited a quarter turn from contact. She slid the pen clip into the gap and felt it wedge. The striker held. Her breath did not.

She let the lid fall softly and moved for the escalator with a speed that looked like walking. Over the overhead speakers, a pleasant voice announced that a store was closing in fifteen minutes. Nobody listened. Everyone listened.

Mandy felt something pass under her like a low wave. The string on her wrist twitched and stilled. Her ears did the warble. She tightened her grip on Mercedes's hand for one count, then let go. If it broke, she would sit. She kept moving.

At the escalator base, the backpack sat in shadow where the moving steps disappeared under the plate. Aldina knelt and slid her hand under with two fingers first, then her whole hand, feeling for the shape she did not want to name. She found a taped object and a wire that did not belong to any maintenance kit. She looked at the screw head on the inspection plate. Standard. She took the small wrench from her pocket and turned. The screw came loose on the second try. The plate shifted.

Behind her, someone laughed too loud. A child cried. A song with too much bass leaked from a store two corridors over and made the floor tremble a hair.

Aldina lifted the plate an inch, then two. The taped object stared up at her from its illegal cave. She did not lift it. She slid the pen clip under its strap and held. The backpack strap shifted. The object did not move. She pressed the clip hard. The spring did not give. She felt the hum of the escalator in her forearms.

"Hold," she said into her collar, and meant it for herself.

The man in the worker jacket looked over his shoulder and saw a woman kneeling by the escalator with her hand under the plate. He saw what he needed to see. He lifted his elbow, made his sleeve hide his hand, and touched the radio nub tucked under his cap. Somewhere up on the second floor, a boy in a hoodie turned his head and began to walk away faster.

Mercedes breathed out a curse. "He saw you," she whispered, the words paper-thin. Mandy did not answer. The satchel was gone from her shoulder and still it felt like weight had not left her.

The crowd pressed closer the way it always does when something starts to collect eyes. Small children pointed. A mall guard walked toward the escalation of attention with a face that said he wished he were anywhere else.

The man in the cap stopped at a table and pretended to examine a menu. He was not eating. He would not be here when anything happened.

Aldina's hand held the improvised striker still. Her other hand slid the wrench across to wedge the plate. Aldina drew in one slow inhale and set her jaw around the exhale. "Almost," she said to the plate and the pen clip and the wrong thing under the moving stairs. "Almost."

CHAPTER 17

The numbers burst across Mandy's lock screen without asking,, huge, arterial red, part coordinate, part cost.

The mall's bright air sheared sideways and thinned. Sound turned syrupy; the tiles under her shoes felt like a photograph of a floor instead of a floor. Then her father was there—same jacket, same soft-creased cheeks, same quiet urgency that always undid her. He didn't speak. He never did. He lifted his hand and pointed, not vaguely but with surgical certainty: past the mezzanine, down the line of kiosks—then he jabbed his finger left, a clear path to a spot she felt in her bones.

"Dad," she whispered, but her voice went nowhere.

The world slammed back into one stream so abruptly she gagged. She bent and dry-heaved, acid and fear burning the back of her throat. Lights went too bright. The noise was a slap. Pressure bloomed at the base of her skull; warmth slid from one nostril. Blood, again.

"Mandy." Mercedes's voice built a bridge with her name. "Hey, stay with me."

"I'm here," Mandy rasped. She wiped her upper lip; red streaked the back of her hand. The hallway clock over the shoe store had jumped. Her mouth tasted metallic. She relayed the numbers to Olle in a whisper, as if it hurt to speak.

Olle had her face in his mathematician's sights, like a clock that had just ticked wrong. One white-knuckled hand pinned his notebook to his chest. "It's live," he said, loud enough to cut the food-court din. "If he can reach you, the window's forming now. At least two devices need to be defanged before the mark or it opens anyway."

"What window?" Aldina demanded, already moving even as the question left her mouth. Confusion flared in her eyes but discipline held her body steady. "Speak in words I can arrest."

"A window as in what?" Bilal snapped, jaw set, eyes scanning the crowd the way a man scans for trouble he knows by smell. "Bombs open windows now?"

"Later," Olle shot back, then pointed with quick, crisp angles. "One at the waste-sorting station by the sushi place. Another likely at the base of that escalator, high foot traffic. If they want a triad, a third under a bench along the atrium wall."

"Pen," Aldina said.

Mandy shoved a pen into her palm. "Clip," Aldina added. Mercedes snapped a hair clip open without thinking—of course she did. Aldina cut through the crowd, a clean, slipping-fish line that drew no eyes, and reached the sorting station in ten seconds.

Mandy forced her legs to perform. The red digits ghosted the edge of her vision; the headache pulsed with her heartbeat. Her father's path was still drawn inside her. She turned her head and the world lagged half a beat, like video buffering.

Aldina lifted the sorting-station lid with two fingers and froze just enough to see: a spring-loaded striker and a small metal cup. Improvised, competent. She wedged the pen clip to block the striker, hands shaking in a way they never did at a lab bench. "Local arm," she muttered—more to anchor her breath than to inform anyone—and eased the lid back without sealing it. "One neutralized."

"Second," Olle said, pivoting, eyes mapping geometry and crowd flow. He pointed at the escalator's inspection plate. "They'll tape a battery pack under that lip and run leads along the rib. We don't have time to pop it clean."

"Move them!" Mercedes called from the railing, already rerouting traffic with a body-and-smile barrier. "Downstairs is closed for cleaning, other side's faster!"

Bilal stepped forward from the edge like a man owning a choice he didn't have. "Tell me where," he said to Olle, voice quiet, sharp.

Olle didn't blink. "Under the bench on the west atrium wall. Second panel from the planter. If it's a battery, rip it clean. Don't short the leads. If there's a coil—there probably won't be—don't touch it."

"And if I'm wrong?" Bilal asked.

"Don't be," Olle said.

Bilal ran.

The air shivered again. Mandy pressed a palm to the railing; the floor became a boat for a second. Red digits bled back in.

00:00:41

Her father slid into place at her shoulder like the square of air had always been his. He jabbed down, then left—harder, more urgent. Down. Left.

"Left," she croaked, pointing. "Under the bench. Left."

"I'm on it," Bilal called without looking up from the sprint. He didn't need to see who she was seeing; he could see what she was seeing her point toward.

Aldina reached the escalator base and slid her fingers under the inspection plate. Tape. Wires. "Got you," she breathed, found the battery, braced the plate with a wrench, teased the pack free with the hair clip, and killed the connection. A shoulder jostled her; she didn't flinch. "Clear."

"Two defanged," Olle said, more to make the math obey than to lead.

"What is happening?" Aldina shot back, eyes still on the crowd, muscles prepped for the next sprint. "What window, what 'defanged' before a mark? Speak, kid."

"Short version: if three local blasts align, they act like a geometry problem," he said, mind in two places at once. "A triangle you don't want. Break two corners, no triangle. No triangle, no... bigger thing. I'll explain."

"Bigger what?" Bilal shouted from the far side, dropping to his knees, skinning a shin, skimming fingers under the bench. Tape. Weight. A pack disguised under gum wrappers and a folded brochure. He worked blind, because living in a leash had taught him how to be good at terrible things. "Battery," he yelled. "I've got a battery."

"Rip it—hard," Olle barked. "Don't let the leads short."

Bilal jerked the pack free, tape snapping, breath sawtoothed. He held the battery up with the wires clean. "Done."

00:00:18... 00:00:07...

The red digits smeared, then slid apart like paint in water and vanished. The air came back like oxygen after a tunnel. Mandy's knees buckled; she slid down the railing post and sat hard. The pounding in her head retreated one notch, then another. Blood at her nose thinned from red to pink.

Aldina exhaled too long for a public place, tucked the dead pack into her jacket as evidence she would never log, and pivoted to face them. Her eyes were sharp and furious and confused. "Someone explain 'window' to me in one sentence that does not get me committed."

"And explain how you knew where to point," Bilal added, standing, tape residue on his knuckles. The hardness in his face had settled into something grimmer than swagger. "You went... away. Then you came back and acted like you had a map only you could see. What did you see?"

Mandy swallowed copper and fear. The world finally held still. She looked at Olle. He nodded once: do it.

"I'll give you the short version," she said, voice steadying as she used it. "I see my dad some times. And he isn't a ghost. He's alive in another branch of the world. Not our past. A parallel track. We presume he can't change our past and neither can we. He can only nudge me now. When he reaches me, it opens a kind of... connection. A window. While it's open, I lose time— seconds. That's what the red numbers I see are measuring. Not a bomb schedule. The cost to me... along with coordinates that we assume signal danger zones."

Aldina stared, working the words like evidence she did not want to be true.

"Cross-branch signaling," Olle said, falling into the groove of an explanation he had been building in pencil-smudged margins for days. "Think of two lanes separated by a barrier. He's in the other lane. Every time he waves at us through a hole in the wall, Mandy pays in time. And these blasts? They're not just terrorism. The locations are deliberate. When three small devices fire at mapped nodes, they make a triangle. That triangle helps stabilize a longer 'window' between lanes. Whoever wants that window is using this mall as a substitute triangle."

"For what purpose?" Aldina demanded.

"We don't know yet," Mandy said. "But my dad keeps pointing me at the corners before they close. If we break two, the bigger window can't hold."

Bilal's mouth pulled tight, not quite a frown, not quite disbelief. "And the red numbers," he said, "are what you pay to see him."

Mandy nodded. "It isn't free."

"And you," Aldina said to Olle, a flash of almost-grudging respect through the confusion, "built this in your head and on a school notebook."

Olle didn't smile. "I built enough to keep us breathing."

"Okay," Aldina said, decision snapping into her voice. "I don't have to believe all of it to believe you. Here is what I do believe: the bombs are placed with intent, and people like us keep getting used as parts. If breaking triangles keeps a larger event from happening, we break triangles."

"We already did," Mercedes said, hands still trembling from shepherding strangers. "Can we go before someone decides we look like we did something interesting?"

"Split, stagger exits, meet at C," Aldina said, automatic. Then—because the questions were still in her eyes—she added, "You will both sit and tell me the rest. I will decide what to do with believing it."

Mandy nodded. "We will."

They peeled out of the mall in ones and twos, different doors feeding the same cold sunlight. Outside, winter light had the clarity of glass rinsed in cold water. Mandy and Mercedes found a side exit by the loading docks; the air out there did not smell like sugar.

Mandy braced her palms on her knees and breathed until the world stopped wobbling. "I hate this," she said quietly.

"I hate it too," Mercedes said. "But you were brave."

"I was terrified."

"Same thing right now."

Olle veered toward them with his notebook, not hugging—he never knew how—but standing close enough that warmth registered. "Eighty-eight seconds lost," he said softly. "Water. Sugar. Chair."

"And a new problem," Mandy said. "Whoever is building these triangles will try again. Somewhere with power."

"Node Zero," Aldina said, coming up from another exit, the disabled pack heavy in her inside pocket. "Substation nexus."

CHAPTER 18

The service corridor still smelled like hot metal and cleaner, the air tasting faintly of pennies. They spilled through the fire door, Aldina first, scanning; Bilal close; Mercedes hauling Mandy by the elbow; Olle trotting with his notebook. The door sighed shut and the mall's roar became aquarium-muffled. Concrete underfoot. A strip of winter sky above the loading docks. Blue pallets, a dented yellow bollard, a cage of empty trolleys.

Aldina stopped so abruptly that Olle almost bumped her. She had a folded slip of paper in her fist, creased to soft cloth from a day of being worried, and she was staring past the pallets to the painted numbers stenciled on the dock wall. Her thumb pressed the coordinates she'd copied from Bilal's hand earlier, the ones he'd insisted on writing down so nothing would be traceable: two lines, degrees and minutes, a pinpoint that wasn't random.

"This is it," she said under her breath. "The coordinates." She cut a glance at Bilal. "You brought us to your mark."

Bilal's mouth tightened. "I told you I don't pick the marks," he said. "I deliver." But his eyes swept the dock face, the seam of the breaker panel, the way the access road and delivery bay made a right-angled cup. He knew a chosen place when he stood in one.

"Don't move," said a voice from the shadowed doorway two bays down, low, even, unafraid.

A figure stepped forward. The motion-sensor lights clicked alive and threw a pale spill over the concrete. Kim von Post pushed back her hood; the spiky blue hair took the light like a crown. Same glasses, different eyes, bright, hungry, very tired.

"Ms. von Post?" Mercedes blurted, incredulous. It came out almost like a laugh, the wrong sound for the shape of the moment.

"Kim," the teacher corrected softly. "We can drop titles now." Her gaze settled on Mandy and gentled by a degree. "Mandy," she said, tender as a hand on a fevered brow. "Your father is alive. Not here, not in this branch. But if you want him with you, I can make it happen."

KVP, Aldina remembered the initials in her head. The crumbs of her research were starting to crawl out of the rug, but the whole of it all was still yet to come together.

Heat sparked in Mandy like a struck match. She didn't breathe. She didn't look away. The slip of paper in Aldina's fist made a dry, papery sound as she refolded it without meaning to.

"How," Mandy said. Just that.

"Because the wall between branches thins at mapped nodes," Kim answered, as if they were in her classroom and someone had finally asked the right question. "Because thin walls can be held thinner with power and timing. Because some people are anchors, and the universe listens when they ache." Her glance tipped toward Olle's notebook, as if she could read the web of times and places through cardboard. "And because I've felt it already," she said, a thread of rawness entering the calm. "Not enough. Not for long. But I've seen what reaches back. I've seen my daughter. She died here. There's a branch where that morning missed her. She's eleven there, right now. If I hold the window long enough, I can keep her, just as he has found a way to reach you."

"By planting bombs?" Aldina asked, acid-dry.

"I don't plant," Kim said evenly. "I suggest. Men who crave power do the rest. They think it's territory. The men above them think it's leverage. I think it's geometry." Her eyes never left Mandy's face. "None of you were supposed to be inside it. But you are, because your father chose you, because you are strong enough to bear the cost."

"The cost is her bleeding and collapsing in bathrooms," Mercedes snapped. "The cost is me watching her blink out."

Kim's gaze softened. "The cost is time," she told Mandy gently. "What you lose when he reaches you. I wouldn't ask if I didn't think we could hold it steady, with help."

"Help," Aldina repeated, like the word tasted wrong. "From the kids you're endangering?"

"From the anchor who has already opened three windows no device could buy," Kim said. "From the boy who can see the drift in his head. From the young man with allegiance to a brother, not a cartel. From you, who would break a law rather than bury another father."

Aldina's throat moved. She didn't lower her stance.

Kim took one small step, palms visible. The motion-lights buzzed. "Listen to me, Mandy," she said, the dock tightening around the name. "I am not your enemy. The thing coming eats cities. I am building a bridge out. And your father, " urgency crept in, "he is trying to steer you to the right span. You just need to look."

The air in front of Mandy thinned, as if someone had wiped a window with the flat of a hand. The lights overhead strobed once. The trolleys rattled in their cage as though a truck had passed on an invisible road. Cold climbed into Mandy's mouth and turned sweet.

He was there.

Not blur, dangerously clear. Pores, stubble shadow, the exact crease by his mouth where he hid jokes. The same checked shirt and jacket. The same weary tenderness in eyes that had tucked her in a thousand times in one universe and never in this one.

Mandy made a sound without consonants. The world's edge went bright.

He lifted his hand. The gesture was achingly ordinary, and it undid her. He pointed, as always, toward her phone, toward geometry only she could see. Then he looked at her, asking a miracle, and his lips moved.

For the first time, sound came with him, fragile, thin, as if it had crossed a frozen lake and might crack. "Love you," he whispered. The words were almost not there, the smallest thread and still everything. "Don't... listen... to her."

Mandy's breath hitched into a sob that didn't have time to become sound.

"Overlap... breaks the world," he managed, as if each word had to wrestle its way through two realities to reach her. "Life and death... meant to... coexist, not... merge." His eyes pleaded. "Please."

Kim's breath quickened; she was watching the readouts that only she could feel. "Energy is high. The wall is thin," she said to herself, to the breaker, to the concrete. She crossed to the gray panel beside the dock door, flipped two switches down and one up with practiced speed. Sparks peeled like cold fireflies and haloed her hair. The corridor lights deepened from white to a bass-note amber. Somewhere deep, a transformer sighed.

Aldina moved toward Kim on reflex, command forming; Bilal shifted, choosing angles; Mercedes froze with both hands at her mouth.

Mandy's father stepped one degree closer. She saw the tiny scar at his temple she knew too well. She reached up as he reached down. Their fingers met.

It felt like touching the skin of a brimming glass, the surface tension of the world dipping but holding. A cool pressure; a hum in her teeth; miniature lightning down every nerve of her arm. He was there. He was there.

In her peripheral vision the red numbers telescoped toward her, not climbing, but closing: 00:02:20. 00:02:19. 00:02:18. A deep ringing, not in her ears but beyond them, poured across the dock like thunder in a box.

"Let go," Olle said hoarsely. "Mandy, you have to let go."

She tried. Her hand didn't want to. Her father shook his head, small, helpless, full of apology. "I love you," he breathed again, the barest thread. "Hold your line."

The numbers hit 00:00:00.

Kim tore the last breaker down.

The window snapped like soap film. Shock ran backward through Mandy, a hard shove. Her knees buckled. She caught the dock edge and tasted iron. Blood broke over her lip. The world shuddered and clicked back into one stream.

Silence gasped.

Kim was already pivoting to the hide where Mercedes had stashed the resealed satchel, the decoy they had swapped in the restroom. She slid it out with the economy of someone who had done this in other lives. Buckles. Weight. Her fingers read the sand where core should have been. She didn't blink. "Of course," she murmured. She shouldered the bag anyway. Her gaze skimmed Mandy's blood-lined mouth. Something raw moved behind her control and reset.

"The coil," she said, seminar-calm. "I'll be taking that back."

"No," Aldina said, steel-flat. The ringed device sat heavy in her coat.

Kim's smile was small, the kind a teacher makes when a student surprises her on a test. "You'll try not to." She stepped backward into the half-dark, feet sure, eyes on all of them at once. "Mandy," she added, as if they were alone in a lab, "grief is a compass. Don't let anyone turn it for you." The bay door swung; her steps dissolved into the building.

The alarms inside the mall were thinning now, changing pitch into the register of insurance and paperwork. Outside, sirens Dopplered away and snapped off, one by one, as if someone were merciful with switches.

They didn't decide to walk. Their legs did it. The five drifted down the access road, through a gap in the chain-link, into a strip of winter-yellow grass sloping toward a ditch of brittle reeds. They lay down like kids after practice. The sky was white and shallow. Their breath went out with the same sound.

"Is it over?" Mercedes said, half-laugh, half-prayer. "Oh my God."

No one wanted to break it. The sentence lay over them like a blanket. The coil in Aldina's lap gleamed like a stolen halo. Dry grass whispered. The coordinates on Aldina's paper, that exact dock, that exact corner, felt like a secret the city had finally confessed.

Mercedes rolled toward Mandy and nudged her arm. "Hey," she said softly. "Hey, hero, get up. We should, "

Mandy didn't move.

"Hey." Bright voice, the one you use when you can't yet admit the floor. She shook Mandy's shoulder, gentle, then harder. "Mands. Come on. Don't do this."

Olle sat up too fast and saw snow at the edges of his vision. "Mandy?"

Aldina was already on her knees, the coil slipping to the grass with a thud. Fingers to wrist. Clinical clicked on inside her like a switch. "Pulse," she said tightly. "Fast. Pupils, " a thumb lifted a lid ", reactive. Nosebleed. Here, " hair pushed back, a fine line of blood under the hairline ", capillary break. Overload."

"She lost more time than usual," Olle said, kneeling, hands hovering. "The window was longer. She touched," His breath skipped. "She touched him."

Bilal stood, then knelt, then stood because his body couldn't pick a position that made the world less. "Ambulance?" he asked, too even.

"Move her carefully," Aldina said. To Mercedes: "Stay with her. Talk." To Olle: "Help me lift on my count." To Bilal, the hardest ask: "Watch. If anyone comes, we're 'waiting on family.'"

Mercedes had both of Mandy's hands, small and fierce. "Hey," she whispered, hair making a small tent around their faces. "We're not done, okay? You don't get to check out because your dad broke physics. Wake up. Please." The please fractured.

They carried her like something sacred, Aldina at shoulders, Olle at knees, Mercedes moving backward whispering at her ear. Bilal walked the perimeter, eyes hawk-wide, empty of performance. He didn't look at the coil. He didn't need to. He knew what it meant to win a piece and not the whole.

They eased Mandy into the back of Aldina's gray car. Coffee-and-wipes smell. Olle slid in beside her, buckled her gently, as if fastening could anchor her to this branch.

"Hospital?" Mercedes asked, braced.

"Home first," Aldina decided, that thin strip of sky and those stenciled dock numbers still stamped behind her eyes. "We stabilize and monitor for ten minutes. Then we go." She caught Olle's gaze in the mirror. "You talk to her. You'll hear changes first."

Olle nodded, pale and present. "Mandy," he said, pitching his voice to the note from childhood thunder nights, "they canceled your show. The genius brother saves the day with math and chicken nuggets in the rerun. You can't miss it. Wake up."

Mercedes scrubbed her face and climbed into the passenger seat. Through the closing window she told Bilal, "If you ghost us, I will light you on fire."

His mouth twitched, not a smile. "I'll be where you need me." It surprised him that he meant it.

The car pulled away. The strip of grass by the mall was suddenly empty. The sirens went elsewhere. The city's hum coughed and came back online. A gull circled and made a hinge-sound.

In the back seat, Mandy's fingers twitched once, then stilled. Olle counted in his head, eight, nine, ten, as if numbers could be a raft.

"Come on," he said, the words both command and prayer. "Come on, sis."

Behind them, in the damp rectangle of the dock, nothing in the city felt like that word. Not yet.

EPILOGUE

They let Mandy sleep. Machines made their careful small sounds, and the winter light in the ward window drained from pewter to charcoal. Outside the room, the hospital moved on muffled wheels; inside it, the five of them sat in different kinds of silence, Aldina with the coil in a cloth tote between her shoes, Olle with his notebook open but his pencil still, Mercedes gripping a paper cup like it might run, Bilal standing because sitting made him feel trapped by his own bones.

When the nurse stepped out to log vitals, Aldina tipped her head toward the alcove near the vending machines. "Two minutes," she said, not asking. Bilal followed.

They stood in the shadow of the humming glass. The strip light flickered in a way that would have made Olle look up and count the cycle. Aldina stared at the reflection of her own face, at how tired can make someone look like a relative you never met.

"For a long time," she said, voice quiet, "I needed you dead."

Bilal's jaw worked once. He did not flinch. "I know."

"I kept a wall at home," she went on. "You were on it. Your file. Your photos. I told myself if I could stop you, it would put the world back where it was the night my father didn't come home from his route." She smiled without softness. "Some days, the thought of killing you was all that kept me... moving. Not sane. Just moving."

He swallowed. "I'm sorry," he said. It came out without posture, without the armor of sarcasm. "For whatever part of it is mine. For the rest..." He lifted his hands a little and let them fall, as if to say, I am small inside a large machine.

Aldina nodded once. "You are not the machine," she said. "That is the mistake I made. I won't make it again."

He let out a breath he had been rationing. "I need help," he said, finally turning to look at her full-on. "I want out. My brother... I cannot lose him. If I talk, if I point, will you protect him? Will you—" he searched for a word he had not used with police before, "—protect us?"

"Protection is not absolution," Aldina said. "I can get you in a room with people who can move your brother, change your phones, reroute your life. I can put my name on that request. But you will tell everything. No poetry. No codes. You will be a witness, not a ghost."

His eyes shone for an instant with something like fear and something like relief. "I can live with that," he said. "I don't know if I can live with anything else."

"Good," she said. She tilted her head, studying him, and for the briefest moment she saw her father's tired kindness in a stranger's face and felt the ache of misdirected fury recede a fraction. "One more thing," she added. "If you hurt those girls, if you even think about using them again, I will take the badge off and meet you where there are no cameras."

He nodded once, solemn. "I won't."

Down the corridor, a soft commotion rose—heels on linoleum, a laugh smothered. Mercedes had stepped out too, wiping her face with the cuff of her hoodie. She saw Bilal and froze; then she moved toward him like you walk into cold water: fast, before your body can change its mind.

"Why are you like this?" she asked, no hello. It came out raw, the question of a girl who had been pulled forward and pushed back too many times by the same hand.

"Like what," he said, but it wasn't a challenge. He sounded tired.

"Hot and cold," she said. "Nice and not. You act like you don't care, and then you help us out like you're ordering a pizza. You tell us not to die, then you point us at the place where people die."

He looked at the floor. "Because I am two people," he said, and it surprised him that the truth could be that small. "One of them is scared all the time, and the other one pretends not to be."

"That's not an answer."

"It's the only one I have without telling you things that make you a target," he said. He risked a glance at her and found her watching him like she was learning a new language and trying to decide if it was worth the effort. "I was good at taking care of someone before I was good at anything else," he added. "Sometimes I forget how to do anything that isn't that. Sometimes I do things I hate because I run out of options." His mouth twisted. "That doesn't make me safe."

She snorted, wiped at her face again. "You noticed my drawings," she said, abruptly changing the ground because feelings made her itch. "On Insta. You liked two. Then you unliked one."

He blinked, startled. "I thought it would... send a wrong message."

She huffed a laugh despite herself. "Everything you send is a wrong message." She took one slow step closer. "For the record," she said, voice dropping, "you do not get to be my tragedy."

His face did something like a smile and then refused to be one. "Good," he said. "You deserve someone boring."

She rolled her eyes so hard it broke the tension. "Get out of here," she said, softer than the words. "Before I change my mind about lighting you on fire."

He nodded. He was still there, though, when they heard the nurse call from Mandy's room and all three of them moved at once.

∧∨∧

Mandy dreamed of fields.

Dry winter grass pressed along her forearms, the smell sweet and old. It was the verge behind the mall, but emptied of noise and sirens, the sky wide as an unasked question. She felt light and heavy at once, like a kite with a short string.

He came the way he always came in dreams and in windows: as if he had been there a moment ago and she had only just remembered to look. He knelt beside her, and his knees made two small dents in the flattened grass. He cupped the air above her temple without touching, the way you do when you want to fix something delicate and know that if you press it will break.

His mouth moved. For a second, no sound; then a word found its way through: not a name, not a warning. It was smaller and larger than both. It was simply, "Stay."

Her eyes filled. He lifted his hand and pointed, not at her phone, not at herself, but toward the city's edge, where pylons were black stitches against the sky. He indicated the substation, the place Olle had labeled Node Zero on a map with an ugly circle that made her stomach turn.

He faded the way mist does under sun: not gone, but no longer where you can hold it. She looked up and saw Aldina standing at the slope's crest, hands in the pockets of her coat, watching the horizon like it had confessed a secret. When she met Mandy's eyes, she nodded once. "Node Zero wasn't the only plan," she said. Her voice carried like a line thrown over water. "We just stopped the small one."

Mandy tried to say *I know*, tried to say *We're not ready*, tried to say *I'm so tired, Dad*. The dream took the words and folded them carefully and put them somewhere she couldn't reach.

∧∨∧

She woke to beeping, to the papery drag of a blanket across her wrist, to the thin ache behind her eyes that meant she had paid another toll. The room was both too full and just right: Mercedes in the visitor chair with her knee bouncing and her mascara smudged into something almost punk; Olle at the bed rail with his notebook open and three columns labeled with equations; Aldina standing like a sentry at the foot of the bed; Bilal in the corner where shadows made him look like a bad idea and a good intention at the same time.

"Hi," Mercedes whispered, like a secret. "You scared me so bad."

"Sorry," Mandy croaked. Her lip tasted of old blood and hospital air. She tried to smile and her face remembered how.

Her phone, facedown on the tray, buzzed. Just once, like a throat clearing. Nobody touched it. It buzzed again, flipped itself on, and the lock screen dissolved into the numbers.

72:00:00

They were huge and red and unapologetic. They burned in the clean light of the hospital room. There was no overlay shimmer, no private trick of sight. They were simply there, on a screen anyone could see.

For the first time, everyone leaned in at the same second and saw the same thing.

Olle's face drained in a way that made him look even younger. "That is a new schedule," he said, voice very steady and very small. "We are not looking at the old drift. This is a fresh cycle. Bigger window. Longer horizon."

"Seventy-two," Aldina repeated, as if committing the number to a ledger. "What does that mean?"

"We don't know yet," Olle said. "But the last triangle wanted a center. This one will want one too."

Far away, muted by glass and distance, a siren wound up and then fell away. The overhead light flickered once and held. Out beyond the hospital, over rooftops and crane arms, the sky did a thing that did not belong to the weather. A faint auroral ripple, pale and quick, combed the clouds and was gone, like hairline cracks appearing and then pretending they hadn't.

Mercedes reached for Mandy's hand under the blanket and squeezed, hard. "Okay," she said, breath hitching into bravado. "Round two."

Bilal looked at the door as if mapping the routes they would need to survive the next three days. "Tell me what to do," he said to no one and everyone.

Aldina's shoulders squared. "We plan," she said.

Mandy stared at the digits until they blurred and resolved again. She felt the steadying weight of her brother's hand on the rail and the ridiculous comfort of Mercedes's chipped nail polish. In her chest, fear and something like hope occupied the same chair and couldn't figure out how to share.

Outside, a crosswalk timer on the street below stuttered and the room's heart monitors kept time with a world that pretended to be simple.

Mandy closed her eyes for one breath and opened them again. The night felt far away and right here. The beginning rhymed with the end. The end rhymed with the beginning.

"Okay," she whispered, to the room, to the phone, to the thin places in the air. "We hold our line."

Publishing Partner: